BLACK CAT MYSTERY Magazine

VOL. 1, NO. 2　　　　　　　　　　　　　　**SPRING 2018**

FEATURES

NEW STORIES

CLASSIC REPRINT

FROM THE CAT'S PERCH

Welcome to the second issue of *Black Cat Mystery Magazine!*

The first issue of pretty much any magazine is always a little misleading. It usually takes a few issues to find a voice and achieve its editorial vision.

The *Black Cat*, though, found its footing almost immediately, thanks to the support of many, many great writers. We found it quite difficult to choose among all the fine stories that crossed our transom. We selected the first two issues simultaneously, and we ended up filling both in a matter of weeks, rather than the months we thought it would take. There were simply *too many* excellent submissions. We could easily have accepted two or three times as many stories as we ultimately chose.

This tell us not only that we're on the right track, but that there is a real need for an additional magazine in the field right now. The existing market isn't large enough to publish everything worth publishing. Not by a long shot.

As with our first issue, we find our tastes gravitating to stories that are not only well written (of course!), but often a little darker, a little edgier than you will find in other magazines today. We hope you will enjoy them and continue on this exciting journey of discovery.

And we promise the next issue won't take nearly as long to appear, as we launch into our regular quarterly schedule as of this issue.

Happy reading!

—John & Carla

Staff

PUBLISHER

John Gregory Betancourt

EDITORS

John Gregory Betancourt

Carla Coupe

WILDSIDE PRESS SUBSCRIPTION SERVICES

Carla Coupe

PRODUCTION TEAM

Sam Cooper

Steve Coupe

Shawn Garrett

Helen McGee

Karl Würf

THE CLEANSING SOIL
Charlie Hughes

I followed Gethyn through the door, and the heat of the pub smothered me. A blanket of warm, stale air draped over the sepia decor.

I spotted them in the corner, sitting around a small circular table, leaning in to speak, their heads almost touching. It should have been a commonplace sight—scruffy, middle-aged men, chatting in a pub—but there was something amiss. I knew it, even then.

One of them, a heavyset lump with huge hands and an ugly bald patch, jabbed his finger at the table as he spoke.

Opposite him, a biker or a heavy metal obsessive—I always struggle to tell the difference—listened intently. He had a thick, long beard and a black tee-shirt clung to his flabby arms. Next to him sat a smaller man with unhealthily pale skin and patchy stubble.

As soon as he saw us approaching, the big guy stopped speaking, mid-flow.

Gethyn introduced me by my user name, "Gino," adding only that I was "…the metal detector I told you about."

The big, bald guy was Christopher. The little one and the biker were Jinks and Fenton, respectively. Gethyn went off to fetch our drinks, and I took my seat.

"So," I said. "What's the big mystery?" I couldn't suppress a nervous laugh.

Jinks sneered. "Something funny?"

Christopher raised his palm. "Easy, Jinks." We remained in silence until Gethyn returned with the drinks.

They all waited for Christopher to speak. "So you like looking for things?"

"I like finding them."

He sniffed. "How'd you get to hear about us?"

I looked at Gethyn. "I thought he'd explained?"

Christopher shook his head. "I want you to tell me."

"Gethyn," I said. "He picked me up from a metal detecting chat board, on a thread about current affairs. He put something up about the wife and daughter who went missing in Milton Keynes, the ones where everyone knew the husband was dodgy." They all nodded.

"He said they might be buried in Wynton Forest. He had all these theories about why they would be there. The distance from the home, the soil, the isolation, all that jazz."

Christopher smiled. "Yes, Gethyn has his theories."

"I thought it was smart, the way he put it all together, so I replied to see what else he had to say. That was it, for a week or two. Then I got a private message asking if I wanted to meet up with a few people. Some experts."

The biker, Fenton, piped up. "So you think you can just turn up and join us?"

"Join what?" I said and turned to Christopher.

"We could tell you, but where's the fun in that?" He downed the remains of his pint and stood. "We'll show you."

* * * *

We followed them in Gethyn's car.

I exhaled. "I'm not sure about this. It's not personal, you seem like a decent guy, but this isn't what I was expecting."

"Stick with it. You got anything better to do today?"

Once, I'd been the guy who jumped at the chance to share my plans. Science Museum with the kids, a surprise birthday dinner with my wife, a weekend away with the boys. I was Mr. Nauseatingly Fucking Conventional, and I didn't mind letting you know it.

That was Before.

Before, I didn't need to scout around on internet chat boards for the pleasure of human company.

After a few more miles we turned onto a remote country road and parked next to some woods. By the time Gethyn and I had joined the others, they were taking shovels out of the boot.

"And they're for?" I said.

Jinks and Fenton exchanged a look, but remained silent. Gethyn put his arm around my shoulder and said, "Gino, you're gonna love this."

The light began to drop and a mild chill entered the air. We walked into the woods, Jinks scurrying alongside Christopher to guide the way. In time, the trees became more dense, the ground underfoot more difficult. Fenton tripped on a fallen branch and Gethyn helped him up. None of the men spoke, except for Jinks's occasional directions.

After twenty minutes, Christopher halted and turned to face me.

"Gino," he said, the others gathering around. "Let me ask you a question. What's your greatest discovery? Metal detecting or otherwise.

What's given you the biggest buzz?"

I hadn't been expecting the question, but I answered without hesitation. "Greenock, 1992. I was on a weekend trip with my club. There were twenty of us staying at the hotel in town. We'd been covering fields near the site of an old fort when I found seven Saxon coins, the club secretary stood by my side."

"A beautiful moment, wasn't it?"

"I was eighteen, and I'd beaten them all."

"A proud discovery, but humbling also. Am I right?"

I'd never heard it put that way before. "Yes. Humbled by the objects, by the passage of time."

He nodded. "You're close. To the beauty. The objects and passage of time, they are wondrous but only for one reason. Which is…?" He raised a finger in anticipation.

I shrugged. He tilted his head, the teacher humouring a child.

"The mystery. The human mystery of how those objects came to be in that particular place at that particular time. How had they been lost? Who lost them, and why?"

I smiled. "Yes."

"So," Christopher continued. "You asked why we're all here. Well, those treasures, those mysteries, the human stories, they come in many forms. Our little team, we seek out the rarest of treasures. Objects which hold the most dramatic of mysteries."

"What would that be?"

He pointed to the ground. "Take two steps to your left."

I looked and saw the grass growing in a rectangular shape, thinner than the ground surrounding it. The soil had been churned, then left. I stepped across and stood on top.

"You are standing on one of our greatest finds."

Jinks whispered under his breath, "Me. I found it."

Christopher placed his hand on the little man's shoulder. "Fine work, Jinks. Fine work."

He turned back to me. "We don't move them, we leave them in their proper place. Twenty-five years I've been doing this. Slowly, very slowly, our group has grown. We've found only eight of them. Eight precious treasures."

Christopher glanced at the others and something passed between them. Without another word, they began to dig.

I stood back. By that point I knew, but still didn't believe. Part of me thought someone would jump out from behind a tree to declare the joke.

Christopher spoke again, but this time not at anyone in particular, his voice raised to the boughs.

"Last year there were five hundred and seventy-four murders in this country and seven hundred and twenty-three people officially went missing. In the vast majority of these cases the body was located and/or the missing person found."

He paced around the others as they dug. "By our calculations, and Jinks deserves much of the credit for this, we estimate that across all these cases, you can expect nought point four per cent to produce an illegal grave which has not been located by the relevant authorities.

"Doesn't sound like much, does it? But that equates to five per year. Over the last fifty years alone that means we have two hundred and fifty bodies hidden on this small island. You'd take those odds when looking for a hoard of Saxon treasure, wouldn't you?"

"I don't look for bodies."

"Don't sneer, not yet. Wait and see." He pointed at the men digging.

The edges of plastic sheeting appeared in the earth and the men became more careful in their excavation. They used smaller spades to clear the soil around the packaging.

I saw the outline of the thing, its size and approximate shape. I couldn't take my eyes off it.

When the sheeting was fully exposed, Christopher produced a Stanley knife and knelt next to it. The others gathered 'round and I joined them. There was total silence. He cut open the top of the bag, then sliced at a right angle, lengthways. After a short pause, he pulled back the sheet to reveal his treasure.

The vile, rotting stench was immediate and overpowering. All of the them covered their faces with handkerchiefs or rags. They'd come prepared. I wrapped my forearm around my mouth and nose, but it made little difference.

She'd been young, in her twenties, perhaps. The skin had browned and decayed and there were clumps of black hair still clinging to the scalp. The eyes had gone, revealing deep, black skull sockets.

"Who is she?" I asked.

Jinks answered this time. "Sally-Anne Parfitt. Brummy lass. She disappeared months ago."

I recalled the news reports. She went missing after a night out with friends in the city. The man who left the club with her claimed they'd parted on the banks of the canal. There had been speculation about him, but the police found no body, nor evidence of foul play.

"How did you...?"

Jinks didn't wait for me to finish. "He's from 'round here, the guy they suspected. Two miles in that direction, on top of the hill, is his parents' house. He couldn't just make a body disappear in the middle of the city. So I tracked him."

"You followed him?"

He smiled. "No need for too much elbow grease these days. Gethyn helped me. With a trojan email we got a geo-tracker onto his smart phone. Then I sat back and watched where the fucker went. For the first few months, nothing. But after it all died down, when he thought it was safe, he came out to these woods. Checking, making sure his treasure was safe.

"Then all I had to do was get hold of the GPR and the rest is history."

"GPR?"

"Ground Penetrating Radar. It used to cost a bomb, only universities and the police had them. Now you can get one on Amazon."

I took two steps back. "And you've kept this from the police and the family?"

Fenton didn't like my tone. "Do you see a blue light on my head? This is… It's…"

"Art," Christopher said. "Art which can only be appreciated by a select few."

I decided not to push any harder. "So now we cover her up and go?"

Christopher was back in control. "Not quite. We've taken a risk here. We've put a lot of trust in you. So we need some guarantees."

The group tightened around me.

"I won't say a word."

Christopher nodded. "You seem sensible. But we've had fools in the past. It gets ugly."

"You have my word."

"Yes, and that's good. But I need something else. I need a picture."

"A picture?"

"A little induction photo for the club records."

"I'll send you one," I said.

"You and her." He pointed at the body. "A moment of weakness, and you blab. We can't have that. A picture keeps it simple."

Gethyn and Fenton had their hands on my back. They pushed me towards the body. Christopher took a phone out of his pocket. "Now kneel next to her. Put your thumb up and smile."

They shoved me down. "No way," I said.

Before I had the chance to move away, I heard a click and the felt cold metal of a gun barrel on my neck.

Christopher raised his eyebrows. "Kneel, smile, thumbs up."

* * * *

There's something wrong with me, I know that.

Normal people don't discuss the location of dead bodies in internet chat rooms. Well-adjusted middle-aged men don't meet with complete strangers because they've been promised "a peek at the dark side of the curtain."

I should have been worried sick, but in the days that followed, it wasn't the gun or their threats which played on my mind. For a man who's already fallen from grace, such things are less important.

I *was* preoccupied with their swagger, their confidence. These were men doing something dangerous and wrong, and for what? Nothing but the buzz of finding the darkest of secrets. I'd been metal detecting all my life and never even suspected such a group existed.

I continued with my life, following the same depressing routines. At work, a machine parts factory on the outskirts of Darlingscote, I was despised by my colleagues. The incident with my wife had put noses out of joint.

Each night I returned home to an empty house and ate meals in front of the TV. I still had another six months of my course to attend, so on Wednesday I went to the group meeting at the local college. Sixteen men sat in a circle of chairs, talking about their demons.

When it was my turn to "share," I invented a story. I'd challenged a young man in a restaurant, I said, over lascivious comments he'd made to the waitress. Almost in tears, I claimed the experience had been empowering and indicative of the progress I'd made. The tutor lapped it up.

A full week after my outing in the woods, I was sat on the sofa, lost in my phone screen, when I received an email from "christie77@gmail.com." It contained only a short message: *Gino, you have been granted level four access to The Cleansing Soil Forum. Click here to verify.* Followed by a link.

My finger was hovering over the screen when there was a knock at the door. I opened it to find Jinks, standing in the rain.

"Hi," he said. "Can I come in?"

I let him push past and he walked through to the kitchen. He whistled. "You need a woman around the house."

Take-away cartons and rubbish lay everywhere. We stood facing each other.

"What do you want?"

"Just to talk," he said.

"Last time we spoke, someone pointed a gun at my head."

He shrugged. "Don't let that trouble you. It wasn't personal."

"What do you want?"

He leaned back on the kitchen table. "I wanted to talk about you. You and the girl in the woods."

I sighed.

"I saw you," he said. "I was watching very closely."

I tensed. "The only reason I haven't gone to the police is that picture."

"You didn't feel it? A little shiver?"

"No," I said.

"C'mon! I saw you. You wanted to jump right in with her!"

I grabbed him by the neck and pushed him back against the table, my face pressed close to his. "Seriously?" I said. "You come into my house and talk to me like that?"

"Easy," he said, but he was smiling. "It's no biggy. We all get it. It's addictive. The hunt, and the find. We found something everybody else had missed."

I held him, but I could feel my resolve faltering.

He went on. "There's other benefits, too, y'know."

I let go and stepped back. "What benefits?"

"Things must be tough for you," he said, gesturing around the kitchen. "Single man, big house. Wife took a chunk out of you, right?"

"Do you want me to lose my temper again?"

"I'm just saying, you think we let him get away with it?"

I said nothing. Jinks put his hand into his tracksuit pocket, pulled out a wad of notes and placed it on the kitchen counter. "A grand. And there's more where that came from."

I took a moment. "Tell me more."

He rested back onto the table. "We called and told him we knew he'd been a naughty boy. We told him we had pictures of him returning to the body. First, he tried to front it out. Then we sent him the pictures. Eventually Christopher got a meeting."

"And he paid?"

"Fifty thousand, lump sum. And there'll be more. His dad's rich."

"They'll just keep paying?"

"They think it's all over. It isn't."

A twitch above my right eye flared. "The money. What are the strings?"

"No strings. Just a little welcome present. More if you stay involved."

"What does that mean?"

He said, "You got an email, just now."

"Yes."

"Take a look."

We sat in silence for a short while. My thoughts drifted, not to the money, but the girl.

"Have you got more…projects?"

Jinks laughed. "Oh yes. We're getting better."

"Like how?"

Jinks stood up. "Click on the link." He smiled and walked out the door.

* * * *

That night, I sat at my PC and entered the online world of "The Cleansing Soil."

You couldn't call it a "club," but it wasn't a cult either. "Secret Society" sounds too *Da Vinci Code*. Men who like looking for, and talking about, dead bodies. There is no name for it. The thread which ran through everything was hunting down the next prize.

Apart from the subject matter, it looked like any other website for enthusiasts. There was a chat room, a live projects page, latest news, and a "trophy room." People chipped in with ideas and there were photos posted of recent expeditions, updates from people chasing down leads.

I'd guess at around thirty active members on the site, all men. Four of them, Christopher, Fenton, Gethyn, and Jinks, had level one access. Only they could see the trophy room and had permission to start new project pages.

The hierarchical system was frustrating, but smart. Different levels made you want to get more involved and turn up to their "treasure hunts," as they called them.

* * * *

The week after Jinks's visit, I drove to Devon with a spade in the back of my car and the address of a car park in Exeter programmed into my sat nav. A level two member called Neale Swinton had arranged for a hunt near the home of a local farmer whose wife had disappeared a year before. Old-fashioned surveillance had confirmed the farmer repeatedly returned to a river path just south of Exeter.

When I got there, the mood could not have been more different to my initial encounter. Gethyn and Fenton were both in attendance and they greeted me with genuine warmth. The sun was out, and we enjoyed the walk from the roadside to the river, Neale directing us along the way. Some of them looked around with metal detectors. Jinks had the GPR. The rest of us scanned the area for disturbed soil.

We found nothing, but the mood remained positive. Some of the guys knew each other well, yet they took the trouble to include me in their chatter. We were on the verge of packing up and going to the pub when an agitated Neale came rushing up the river path.

"It's him. It's the bloody farmer. He's coming."

Jinks was first to respond. "Take it easy, everyone. We're metal detecting on public land."

A man wearing heavy boots, carrying a pair of walking poles, came 'round the bend in the river. We'd grouped ourselves around the detectors, pretending not to notice him. When he reached us, he stopped and struck up a conversation with Fenton.

"Lovely day for it," he said.

"Yep," Fenton replied.

"Found anything?" he said, smiling.

"Not today."

"Lovely spot this, y'know. Lovely spot."

"Very nice."

"I used to come here with my wife." The sadness in his voice was palpable.

Fenton could not have looked more uncomfortable.

The farmer continued, "We'd come here every weekend. Go walking with the dogs."

Neale walked over. "Where's your wife today?"

"You'd have to ask her," he said. "Found out last week she'd run off to Spain with a guy from her Pilates class. Police had been looking for her and everything."

I looked around our group. Their shoulders shook as each man tried to suppress fits of mirth.

"Damnedest thing," the farmer said, and walked on.

As he rounded the bend, the damn burst. There were howls of laughter all around.

* * * *

From that day onward, I immersed myself in the group. Since the incident with my wife, I'd withdrawn from everybody I knew, embracing the loneliness. I'd even shunned those close friends who'd refused to abandon me.

But now, for the first time since that night, I felt an affinity with other people. Most of the guys involved with Cleansing Soil were the type who struggled to fit in. They weren't attractive and they didn't have scores of people around them. They had interests and desires that most people struggle to understand. Yet there was a flip side. When we, the outsiders, came together, the bond between us was strong.

I looked forward to the social side just as much as the hunts. Afterwards we'd always find a pub and spend the night talking and joking. Sometimes it was about the search for new treasure, sometimes it was just general talk. We always had to be a little circumspect and nobody used their real names. I enjoyed the camaraderie no less for it.

By November that year, I was getting along to hunts every Saturday and Sunday. Most evenings I spent my time in front of the computer, exchanging messages with other members and checking for updates on the various projects.

We were all excited to hear about the Christmas party Christopher was organizing. He'd booked a table at a posh hotel in Birmingham, with the bill covered by group funds.

I took the day off work and caught the train. We had a large room to ourselves and all the guys made an effort to look the part. Christopher and the other level ones sat at the top of the table. I sat in the middle, next to Neale and some of the others. The big man made a speech about what a great year it had been. Jinks's historic find and three new trustworthy members added to our ranks. He mentioned each of us by name.

He spoke in euphemisms, mining it for humor at every opportunity. He referred to "grave developments in the Warwickshire area" and "issues in the North which had been buried for too long." Some laughed and others groaned, but he judged it well. There was great affection in the room for our leader.

The only sour note from his speech was an omission. Christopher praised the support he'd received from the other levels ones, except for Fenton, who sat at the end of the table looking uncomfortable in a grimy white shirt and gray tie. I wasn't the only one to notice it.

The meal turned into a pub crawl as we streamed out into the middle of Birmingham. When we left the second pub, I was about to follow the others further into New Street when I felt a hand on my shoulder. It was Gethyn.

"Gino, would you join us in a place 'round the corner? Christopher wants a word."

I looked behind him and saw Jinks and Christopher looking over at us.

"Sure. Let's go."

We settled down in a quieter pub called the Tap and Spile.

The mood was still relaxed, but I wanted to know more. "So what's this all about?"

Christopher said, "Gino, I'm impressed. That's the first thing I wanted to say. Everybody can see what an asset you've become to us. You're there, front and center at the hunts and you offer wise counsel on the forum. If I'm honest, I can't say I was optimistic when we first met. But I'm pleased with how it's turning out. Very pleased."

Before I could thank him, Gethyn interjected, "If you check your email, you'll see that I've just given you level two access."

I smiled. "Going up in the world."

Gethyn continued, "You can organize your own projects now. You can lead others."

Christopher said, "You've earned it." Then he leant back in his chair and took a deep breath. "That's not all we wanted to speak about."

The three men looked at each other and then back at me. Jinks said, "We've got a problem."

"What sort of problem?"

Christopher again. "It's Fenton. He's causing difficulties."

Gethyn added, "He got to level one because of a find. It was a good one, over in Shropshire. Making a find like that gets you to level one, so we brought him into the fold."

Jinks shook his head. "We brought him in and we trusted him. Level one gets you access to the bank account. We each get a little allowance, in recognition of the work we do, but the rest of the spending has to be on projects."

Christopher leaned in. It was the same pose as the first time I'd seen him, jabbing his finger, angered by something the man across the table had said to him. Fenton.

Christopher picked up from where Jinks left off. "He's taken thousands. Wasted it on gambling and trips to Amsterdam. The bastard. Claimed he was doing research whilst spending our money on whores."

Gethyn took up the thread. "So we've decided. It may take a while, but we want to replace Fenton among the level ones."

"Replace him with who?" I asked.

"You."

I screwed up my face. "I need to find one, don't I? I'd need to lead a project and find one for myself."

Jinks said, "And we can help with that. I have ideas. Maybe, in normal circumstances, I'd have chased them down myself. But we need you on board, and we need him out."

Christopher put it on the line. "So we need an answer, Gino. Are you willing to come inside?"

I looked at all three of them. They wanted me, they needed me.

"Yes," I said. "I'll do anything you want."

* * * *

Jinks gave me three leads. A businessman in York who'd gone missing the week after his wedding day, a student at Keele who'd disappeared the night of her Fresher's party, and a market stall holder in Leicester who was mixed up with some unsavory local criminals.

The other members knew I was being groomed for a leadership role. They became more respectful in their conversation with me, both online and in person. I set up hunts, enlisting their help to chase down Jinks's suggestions.

It took months of hard work. Every weekend, and sometimes during the week, I'd pursue his tips. Jinks loaned me the GPR so I could cover more ground. Sometimes I'd search on my own, sometimes with others.

Fenton became noticeable by his absence. He only contributed on the forums and even then it was perfunctory.

After four months with no success, Jinks sent me a text message:

Gino. We have him. I got a track on the student who lived across the hall from Helen Jenkinson, the Keele student. He's been sniffing around in the forest to the south of the campus. No reason for him to go there. He sits on the hill and looks. Get yourself into those trees on Saturday. I'll come and join you if I can. Keep this one to yourself. I think we have something.

I was so excited I rose at 4 a.m. on Saturday morning and drove up the M6 to Keele. It's an open campus, picturesque and modern. As I weaved my way through the expansive grounds, I could see students stumbling home after their night-time exploits. Some alone, but couples, too. Young, happy people embracing life and optimistic about their future.

Before Cleansing Soil, the sight of them would've prompted resentment and bitterness in me. I'd been forced into manual work at a young age and had none of the opportunities they enjoyed. My natural inclination was to dislike anyone who appeared to have had it easier than me.

But not that morning. In a manner I could never have predicted, I was finding my way now, with a group of men who understood and respected me. A sense of pride and status was mine for the taking. Good luck to those kids, I thought, and good luck to me.

I wondered if Helen Jenkinson had experienced the same sense of optimism when she arrived at this place. What kind of future had she wished for, before she'd been placed in the soil?

I parked close to the woods and took my rucksack out of the car. Walking along the paths between the halls of residence and the academic buildings with my spade, I hoped to blend in as a groundskeeper.

I took my phone out and called Jinks to check he was near our meeting point. He answered on the first ring.

"Hi. You there?" he said.

"Almost. You?"

"Bad news. Got stuck in traffic. Accident on the motorway." In the background I could hear movement.

"You coming alone?"

"Yeah," he said. "Have a look around without me. I'm sure it's there somewhere. Start at the eastern end."

At first, some of my good cheer dissipated. I wanted Jinks with me. He had such good instincts and I wanted to share this with him. But as I approached the trees near the old Sneyd Manor, I had a change of heart. Maybe it was better to be on my own. To make the find without help would add to my glory. I could live off this for years.

I looked over my shoulder and entered the woods. The ground was full of mulch and debris, woven together by the damp. Within minutes I was draped in semi-darkness, interrupted by thin shafts of light penetrating the branches high above. In the distance, I could hear the low hum of the motorway.

I was systematic, walking for ten minutes along the eastern edge of the trees until I came to the border, then doubling back. It was after my third sweep that I saw it. A low mound of soil rising from wet leaves.

I felt it again. The steady increase of tension in my shoulders and neck, the quickening of my pulse. I had the instinct now. From thirty yards away, I knew what I was looking at.

A young man had done something terrible to that girl and this is where he'd brought her. In the dead of night, panic coursing through every fiber, he'd dragged her into these dense trees. As I paced towards the grave, I looked at the world as he must have seen it. Desperate to keep his awful secret and salvage his future.

When I reached the grave, it was obvious it would not take long. The kid hadn't taken the time to bury her deep, knowing his only chance was the isolation of the woods. I took my spade and began removing the wet soil. Soon, I saw the black bin bag. I might have ripped it off there and then, but I wanted to savor the moment.

My hands shaking, I scraped the rest of the soil away.

With the bag revealed, I knelt next to the body, my knees almost touching the corpse's head. This was it. Whatever happened now, for the rest of my life, I would have this moment, always know I had uncovered one of the great secrets of the cleansing soil.

I tore away the plastic and froze. Staring back at me, eyes open, tongue protruding to one side, was a man. The idea of Helen Jenkinson's body dissolved, destroyed by the thing before me. It was not supposed to be like this.

Fenton. Fenton was dead.

Before I could process what I was looking at, I felt a hand on my shoulder.

"Thomas Winton. I am arresting you for the murder of..."

The words drifted to nothing.

* * * *

I had a known history of violence and they found things in my house which I could not account for. Large amounts of cash and pictures of Fenton taken, apparently, without his knowledge. Some of them were near his home, others in the red-light districts of Amsterdam. Why did I have these pictures and where had the money come from? My answer, that they had been planted, satisfied nobody.

The police had tracked me all the way to the body. They'd been tracking me for a week following a tip-off. The officer spread out the photos on the interview room table. Fenton and I together, just us. I recognized the scene from the hunt in Devon.

I told them about the Cleansing Soil and they listened, but nobody believed a word I said. I showed them emails I'd received, but when we followed the links to the website, they were dead. No student by the name of Helen Jenkinson had attended Keele University.

The officers were thorough. They checked out the information I had on Gethyn, Christopher, and Jinks, but none of them existed in the real world. Just a playful fantasy for a man who'd killed his friend.

I hoped the grave site they'd shown me on our first meeting would prove my story, but when we got there it was nothing but a mound of dirt. The boys had been thorough, too.

The trial starts tomorrow and I've decided to plead guilty. I have nothing to back up my story and denying it all will just keep me in jail longer. Even as it stands, I'm staring at a twenty-year stretch.

Sitting in my cell, I think of those men, searching for corpses in the ground. The sadness which courses through me is almost unbearable, but I endure. One day, I will be away from here, free to make new treasure of my own.

✗

Charlie Hughes lives in South London. He began writing suspense, horror, and dark psychological short stories three years ago. He's since been published in various magazines and anthologies. His story "The Box" took first prize in the 2016 Ruth Rendell Short Story Competition. "Together" appeared in *Ellery Queen's Mystery Magazine* in March 2017.

SKIRTS
Michael Bracken

George Milonovich did not know if his city was becoming Sodom or if it was becoming Gomorrah, but the increasing number of strip clubs, gay bars, and general perversity he witnessed on a daily basis certainly indicated it was headed in that direction. He still remembered the days when his neighbors kept their predilections to themselves rather than flaunting them in public, and he fondly remembered the days when he didn't have to bite his tongue every time he had a politically incorrect thought. His daughter Tonya, twenty-one years his junior and already pushing hard against fifty, often suggested he was a dinosaur destined for extinction if he didn't adapt to the new world around him. "I'm going to die soon either way," he always told her, "so why bother?"

At that moment, she sat on the other side of his desk, holding a file folder containing a retainer check and a signed contract. Tonya might have been her mother's twin when she was young, and Milonovich often wondered if his wife would have aged as well as his daughter had she lived. Over the years, Tonya had thickened a bit, and regular visits to a salon kept her shoulder-length auburn hair free of gray. She kept her make-up to a minimum, and her nails short and painted neutral colors.

Milonovich was no longer the strapping young man who had wooed and won Tonya's mother. The effects of aging had shaved almost two inches from his height so that when his daughter wore modest heels they stood eye-to-eye. His thick black hair had turned thin and gray, and he kept it trimmed with weekly visits to a barber nearly his own age. Regular trips to the gym—sometimes in the company of his daughter—kept him in shape, but he could no longer chase down leads or break down alibis without getting winded. After listening to Tonya's explanation of the case she had accepted on behalf of Milonovich and Daughter Private Investigators, he said, "We don't handle murders."

"But you found Harold Wainwright's killer last fall."

"That was personal," Milonovich said. Wainwright had suffered a fatal heart attack during an early evening walk in his neighborhood, the result of a mugging that went wrong. Milonovich had tracked down the mugger. "Harry and I went to school together, and the cops weren't doing a thing about it."

"The police aren't doing anything with this case, either," Tonya said. "Our client says they've moved on."

The firm's bank account maintained a healthy balance, as did Milonovich's and his daughter's personal accounts, so they could afford to turn away unsuitable cases. Milonovich wanted to understand why Tonya had accepted this case, so he made her repeat everything she'd already told him.

Peter Tucker had been found in his bed mid-morning one Friday, dead from a single gunshot to the head. The revolver in his hand was registered in his name. No one had heard the shot, but the widow living across the street saw a woman leave the Tucker home around 10:30 p.m. No one else had been seen entering or leaving the home until an intern from Tucker's company discovered the body.

Tonya looked up from her notes. "And no one seems to care that he's dead."

"Except our client."

"Sandra Hellerman."

"What's her connection to all this?"

"Chief Financial Officer of Tucker Pucker Products," Tonya explained. "The company carries a multimillion dollar key man life insurance policy on Mr. Tucker. If it's a suicide, as the police and coroner have determined, the insurance company doesn't pay off. If we can prove it was murder—"

"Then it does."

Tonya nodded.

"And what's Mrs. Hellerman get out of it?"

"Ms. Hellerman."

Milonovich nodded at his daughter's correction.

"She says the company is struggling because of Tucker's death. The intern who found the deceased had loan papers for him to sign, for a loan to be secured by a second mortgage on his home intended to finance an expansion of his company's manufacturing plant. Without his signature, the loan fell through, and the expansion was put on hold," Tonya explained. "The insurance money would resolve those problems."

"So, what does the company manufacture?"

"Have you heard of Fleshlights?"

Milonovich nodded as if he had, but he hadn't.

"Tucker Pucker Products manufactures a competing product." Tonya took the retainer check from the folder and slid it across the desk to her father.

He examined it, counted all the digits to the left of the decimal point, and said, "I guess we can ask a few questions."

* * * *

The next morning, Milonovich put on his best suit—a blue pinstripe—and went to visit Eugena Arquette, the widow who lived across the street from Peter Tucker's former home. A full two minutes after he leaned into the doorbell a second time, a woman near his age who had dressed for the day in tailored tweed slacks, a simple cream-colored blouse, and a single strand of pearls with matching drop earrings, opened the door. Her hair had been expertly styled in a sleek gray bob, and she wore her age without deception. Wearing flats, she looked up at him and shouted, "May I help you?"

As Milonovich handed her one of his business cards and tried to identify himself, she added, "You'll have to speak up. I'm not wearing my hearing aids."

He did, confirmed the woman's identity, and said, "I'd like to ask you a few questions about—"

"It says here you're a private detective. Is that true?"

"Yes, ma'am, it is."

"And what do you think I can do for you?"

Milonovich explained that he had some follow-up questions about her neighbor's death several months earlier.

"Why didn't you say so sooner?" She stepped out of the way and ushered Milonovich into her house. "Coffee?"

"Yes, please."

A few minutes later, after Eugena put on her hearing aids and pushed aside the laptop she'd been using prior to Milonovich's arrival, they sat at the kitchen table and talked over steaming cups of coffee.

"The police interviewed me the day they found the body," she said. "I'm not certain the officer spent even five minutes asking me questions. When you get to be our age—"

She let her sentence hang in the air so Milonovich grabbed the tail end of it. "No one listens. They're too busy trying to get away because they think age is contagious."

"They'll catch it all right," Eugena said, "if they're lucky."

Milonovich laughed politely at her little joke.

His business card lay on the table between them and Eugena tapped it with her finger. Her nails had been manicured recently and painted a light mauve. "You have other children?"

"Just the one daughter," he said. He knew better than to rush anyone of his own generation. That's why he had opted to interview the widow while his daughter spoke with the intern who discovered Peter Tucker's body. "What about you?"

"A son, but he moved to California several years ago and I only see him on the holidays."

"And your husband?"

"Harold? He's been gone a long time now. Cancer, God rest his soul. Your wife?"

"She died when Tonya was six. I had to raise my daughter by myself."

"That must've been difficult."

"You have no idea. Some nights I had to take her on stakeouts, and let her do her homework in the backseat of the car while I was tailing philandering husbands."

"So you made her your partner."

"Tonya was with me so much, I printed business cards for her to give to her friends," he said. "I never expected her to join the firm after college. Now I can't seem to do anything without her."

"Grandchildren?"

Milonovich shook his head. "My daughter never married. Now it's too late."

Eugena reached across the table and patted the back of Milonovich's hand. "That's too bad. I don't know what's worse, though. I have two and I never see them. They don't call, they don't write, and when I call them they don't have time to talk. They tell me if I want to know what they're doing I should check their Facebook accounts."

Milonovich avoided use of the firm's computers, preferring to wear down shoe leather rather than fingertips when working a case. "Seems impersonal."

"Quite, but they don't think so," she said. "How do you keep up with your daughter's life?"

"I see her every day, and she tells me whatever I want to know."

Eugena turned to her laptop, pressed several keys, and examined whatever came up on her screen. "She's a good-looking young woman," she said. Then she looked up. "Do you know she has a friend named Brenda?"

"Her roommate? She's a nurse."

Eugena stared at Milonovich for a moment before she said, "You're a wonderfully old-fashioned man. There aren't many like you left. So, what is it you wanted to ask me, Mr. Milonovich?"

"George," he said. "Call me George." Then he asked her to tell him everything she remembered about the night Peter Tucker died.

"There isn't much to tell," she said. "At ten-thirty-five, I saw a woman on the front porch of Mr. Tucker's house."

"Are you certain of the time?"

"Positive," she said. "The local news had just ended. I had just turned off the television before heading upstairs to bed, and I was removing my hearing aids. That's when I saw her through the front window."

"What was she doing?"

"Leaving."

"And you know this because—?"

"She left," Eugena said. "I watched her walk to the corner."

"Did she get in car, a taxi, one of those Uber things?"

Eugena shook her head. "I don't know. I lost interest and went to bed."

"What did the woman look like?"

"Medium height, medium build, slender hips, perky upstairs, if you catch my meaning. She had dark blond or light brown shoulder-length hair."

"What was she wearing?"

Eugena closed her eyes for a moment. "A red dress. That's what caught my attention. Not every woman can wear a red dress and look good in it."

"And she did?"

"Well, she didn't look bad."

"Anything else you can remember about her?"

"She wore white gloves and carried a Louis Vuitton leather purse."

"You could see that from here?"

"My hearing may be shot, but my eyesight's fine." Eugena winked as she reached across the table and placed her hand on his. "The moment I saw you standing on my porch, I knew you were one-of-a-kind. There aren't many men our age who know how to dress when calling on a lady."

Uncertain how to respond to her obvious flirting, Milonovich asked, "And why is it you were the only person to see this woman?"

"Take a look around when you leave here," Eugena said. "My house is probably the only one on the block with the blinds open. People don't look out because they don't want other people looking in."

Milonovich took that as his cue to excuse himself, and Eugena walked him to the door.

"You have my number," the private investigator said. "Call me if you think of anything else."

"I'll do that," Eugena said with a coy smile. "I certainly will do that."

* * * *

Late that afternoon, Milonovich and his daughter sat in his office again. After he told Tonya everything he had learned from Eugena Arquette, he asked about her progress.

"Other than our client, I haven't met a woman yet who isn't glad Tucker's dead," Tonya said, "but I can't say I've met the one who did him in."

Each semester, Tucker Pucker Products used a different group of six students from the local business school, and Tonya had spent the day tracking down all the interns working at the time of Peter Tucker's death.

"The female interns all refused to be alone with the deceased," she explained. "Austin Stoltz was the only male intern that semester, so when Tucker didn't show up at work and didn't answer his cell phone, our client sent Austin to Tucker's home with the loan documents."

"What time was this?"

"Austin said he arrived around ten-thirty and saw Tucker's car in the driveway. He rang the bell and knocked on the door. After about ten minutes, he tried the knob. The door wasn't locked, so he let himself in and started calling Mr. Tucker's name. When he found the body in the bedroom, he backed out of the house and called 9-1-1 on his cellphone."

"He touch anything while he was inside?"

"He said he didn't," Tonya said. "CSU confirms his story."

"The Crime Scene Unit?"

"I called in a favor," Tonya said. "Remember Anna Kendrick, works in the Crime Scene Unit?"

"You two used to be close. I haven't seen her around since Brenda moved into your place. What happened?"

Tonya didn't answer her father's question. Instead, she said, "CSU didn't lift any prints that seemed out of place. Austin's were on the doorknob and the front door. They also lifted prints from Tucker, his ex-wife, his son, our client, and a woman Tucker had been seeing off and on for about ten years. The only prints on the gun were Tucker's. Anna also told me there were no signs of a struggle. While we were talking, she called a friend in the coroner's office for information about the body. There were no defensive wounds and no signs of trauma—other than the single gunshot wound—to indicate any kind of scuffle. He'd been drinking, though, and he'd had steak, potato, and green beans for dinner a few hours prior to his death."

"What else did you learn?"

"From the interns, quite a bit. They were a talkative bunch. Apparently they're almost invisible and people say things in front of them they might not say otherwise."

"Such as?"

"The deceased's world was falling apart, if the interns aren't exaggerating. That loan he was supposed to sign for? He was putting up his home and some investments as collateral because the company was struggling. That's why he used unpaid interns—to cut costs. A former employee had threatened to sue him for sexual harassment, he had separated from his wife almost a year before his death, their divorce had been finalized only a few weeks earlier, and he had, apparently, recently broken up with the woman he'd been seeing."

"And our client didn't bother mentioning any of this?"

"She hinted that he might be having a few problems, but she said it was nothing that would make her think he was suicidal."

"Anything else?"

"Two of the interns told me about a man who came in and threatened to kill Tucker. Turns out he was the husband of the woman threatening to sue him."

"We have a lot of people to talk to," Milonovich said. "Let's see if we can start with the deceased's wife."

Tonya glanced at her watch. "She lives with her son. So, dinner first? Give them time to get home?"

* * * *

They were a mismatched pair. Milonovich still wore his best suit, but his daughter was dressed in jeans, hiking boots, and a pink polo shirt. They stood on Peter "Sonny" Tucker, Jr.'s front porch, rang the bell, and waited until his mother opened the door. After they identified themselves, Andrea Tucker ushered them into the living room and called to her son.

Several photos lined the fireplace mantle, and Milonovich glanced at them while waiting for Sonny. Several were of mother and son. In a few photos Andrea stood with a blonde who could have been a younger relative, and in others Andrea or Sonny or both of them stood with an older couple who appeared to be her parents. There were no photos of the deceased anywhere on the mantle.

Milonovich turned when Sonny entered the room. Sonny and his mother had a similar height and similar build, and both had short black hair, hers cut in a fashionable bob and his in a close-cropped crew. Sonny settled onto the couch next to his mother and she took his hand.

Tonya settled into a brown suede recliner, so Milonovich took the remaining seat.

Following a few preliminaries, Andrea said, "The coroner told us it was suicide. Why do you think someone killed my husband?"

"We don't think anything," Milonovich explained. "We've been asked to look into your husband's death, that's all, but I am surprised you didn't contest the coroner's findings."

"Why?"

"His life insurance wouldn't pay off for suicide."

"Peter let his personal policy lapse when I moved out of the house. He said he wouldn't give me a dime living or dead," Andrea said, "and he was true to his word."

"How's that?"

"He changed his will when we divorced. I didn't receive a thing."

"My mother tolerated his philandering and abusive behavior for years," Sonny said, interrupting his mother, "until I convinced her to leave him. She's better off here with me. Much better off."

Milonovich saw Andrea squeeze her son's hand before he directed his attention to Sonny. "And you? You had nothing to gain from his death?"

Sonny shrugged. "Cut out of his will, just like my mother, but he's out of our lives. Or, he was until you two showed up."

"What about his company?"

"Incorporated. My father's shares went to the dyke who kept the books."

Milonovich glanced at his daughter. "Sandra Hellerman, the CFO?"

Andrea said, "Surprised me, too. She might be the only woman whose pants he didn't try to get into."

Before Milonovich could ask another question, his daughter took over. "So where were the two of you the night Mr. Tucker died?"

"We've been over all this with the police," Sonny said.

"So, humor us."

"I went to dinner with an old friend," Andrea said. "She brought me home around ten."

Tonya turned to the dead man's son. "And you?"

"I went to a show downtown."

"Alone?"

"Yes."

"Anyone see you there?"

"I'm certain they did, but I don't know if they would recognize me."

"And what time did you get home?"

"Must've been close to eleven."

She turned to Andrea. "So you were here when your son returned?"

"I was reading in my room when I heard him come in."

"Your husband was killed with a .38," Milonovich said. "Did you know he owned a gun?"

"He had that things for years," she said. "He kept in the nightstand, said he was afraid of burglars."

"Burglars?"

"You've seen the house, I presume, and the neighborhood. Fifteen, twenty years ago, there was a string of break-ins. Some of the neighbors purchased home security systems. My husband bought a gun."

He looked at Sonny. "So you both knew about the gun?"

"Of course," Sonny said. "I was a still a teenager when he brought it into the house."

After Milonovich thanked them for their time, Andrea showed the two private investigators to the door. As he and his daughter were stepping onto the porch, Milonovich turned. "One last question," he said. "Do you own a Louis Vuitton purse?"

"I own three, actually." She glanced back at her son. "Why?"

"No reason."

In the car on the return drive to the office, Milonovich asked, "Don't you think it's a little strange that Andrea Tucker lives with her son?"

"She moved in with him when she left her husband."

"And they're still living together? That must crimp his dating life. What man wants to bring a date home knowing his mother's there waiting?"

Tonya said, "I lived with you until I was thirty-two, and—"

"—and you certainly didn't bring any men home to meet me. You kept that part of your life to yourself, didn't you?"

* * * *

The next day, Milonovich put on his best suit and visited Corby Nelson, an auto mechanic who had threatened Tucker in front of two interns, while his daughter visited Cathy Nelson, the former Tucker Pucker Products employee who had threatened a sexual harassment suit against Tucker. Corby stood a full head taller than Milonovich, sported a full beard, and wore greasy overalls. The private detective developed a crick in his neck from looking up at the taller man as they spoke.

"I understand you threatened Peter Tucker."

"If that coward had come out of his office, I would have pounded him into the ground for what he put my wife through."

"You know he's—"

"Dead? Yeah, I know. Killed himself, the coward. Couldn't face up to the things he'd done."

"Such as?"

"You think my wife was the first woman he harassed? I doubt it. I think she was the first woman who stood up to him and—"

"Harassed? How did Tucker harass you wife?"

"Inappropriate comments, touching her in places no gentleman touches a woman without her consent, suggesting that raises and promotions would come her way if she slept with him."

"And she rebuffed his advances?"

"When Cathy finally had enough, she quit. When she was denied unemployment benefits because of him, that's when I lost it. That's when I went down there to tear his head off."

"But you never saw him?"

"I was stopped by a couple of young women working in the front office. They told me Tucker had gone for the day, but I knew he was there and I demanded to see him. Instead, they had me talk to another woman—a blonde who said she was the CFO—"

"Sandra Hellerman."

"That sounds right," Corby said. "She suggested we might be able to reach some kind of settlement. A few weeks later, after meeting with my wife, they did reach a settlement: Twenty thousand dollars for my wife to withdraw her challenge to the denial of her unemployment benefits and to stop threatening legal action. Hellerman later hooked my wife up with a job at a women's shelter, of all places."

Milonovich pondered that for a moment and then asked, "What's your wife look like, Mr. Nelson?"

"She's—no, here, let me show you." He pulled out his wallet and showed Milonovich a photograph of his wedding. Though Cathy looked quite small next to Corby, she was medium height, medium build, and blond.

"You think your wife might still be harboring some resentment against Mr. Tucker?"

"Hell, we both are, but the police already talked to us about this. We were together the night he died."

"Anyone else see you?"

"We were at home. So, no."

Milonovich thanked Corby and made to leave. Then he paused. "One more thing," he said. "Does your wife own a Louis Vuitton purse?"

"I don't know. What's it look like?"

"You'd know if she did," Milonovich said. "They cost more than my first car."

* * * *

Milonovich met his daughter for lunch at the Greek diner down the block from their office. Over gyros they compared notes. The Nelsons told the same story.

"Cathy says she's moved on," Tonya said. "Working at the shelter gives her the opportunity to help women in situations far worse than hers."

"Her husband certainly hasn't," Milonovich said, "but he doesn't fit the description of the woman seen leaving Tucker's house that night."

"She does, and he's her alibi."

"What about the purse?"

"She says she does own a Louis Vuitton, but it's a canvas clutch she bought at a high-end resale shop with the money from the settlement. She doesn't think her husband knows about it."

"Why?"

"From the way Cathy Nelson talked, her husband sounds a little controlling, and jealous when other men pay attention to her."

"Turns out he had good reason to be with Tucker."

"Anyhow, she says she's glad to be working in a place with just women."

After they finished lunch and were walking back to the office, Tonya said, "Can you meet with Nikki Wilson by yourself? I have something important to do this afternoon."

* * * *

Milonovich met Nikki Wilson at her home, less than a mile from where Peter Tucker died. She was a diminutive brunette who had started seeing Peter Tucker long before his wife walked out, and she wasn't shy about anything. She wore a short red skirt and a sheer white blouse with nothing beneath it. Her lips and her fingernails were painted bright red, and her make-up had been applied a little too heavily, as if she had been attempting to mask the signs of middle age.

She guided Milonovich into her living room by placing a hand on his elbow and leaning into him so that one breast pressed against his side. She settled him on a leather recliner and settled onto the couch in a position that allowed the mid-day sun filtering through the window to turn her blouse even more translucent.

After some preliminaries, and despite the distractions, Milonovich asked, "What was your relationship with Peter Tucker?"

"That's my pucker on all of Peter's products," she said. "Without me, he'd have nothing."

Milonovich wasn't interested in her pucker, so he asked how long she had known him.

"We met about ten years ago, in a strip club of all places."

"Were you—?"

She shook her head. "Me? Never, though I had the body for it." She sat up straighter and thrust her chest forward. "Still do. I was there with one of his suppliers, a guy who wasn't worth my time. I left him that night to hook up with Peter."

"You knew he was married?"

"Sure, but what did I care? He had money and he was willing to spend it on me."

"I understand Mr. Tucker didn't treat women well, yet you continued seeing him—"

"Yeah. Ten years, give or take, and, no, he didn't. But as his sidepiece I didn't have to put up with him the way his wife did. Things changed when she walked out. He thought I should be the next Mrs., but when I learned his company was in trouble, he was having trouble paying his bills because attorney fees had drained his bank account, and that he was more show than go, I decided it was time to move on. We went to a late-evening dinner at The Cattle Baron's Club the night he died, and that's when I ended it. I told him we were finished and that I never wanted to see his sorry ass again. I didn't think he'd blow his brains out because of it."

"You think he committed suicide because you dumped him?"

"Hell, I don't know why Peter committed suicide, but maybe my dumping him was the last straw. After all, what man could live without these lips?" She puckered up and blew a kiss in Milonovich's direction.

He didn't react to it. "So, you're convinced Tucker committed suicide?"

Nikki leaned forward and licked her lips. "You're thinking he was murdered? That would be delicious."

"I'm just asking a few questions." Milonovich stood and made to leave. Then he paused. "One more thing," he said. "Do you have a Louis Vuitton purse?"

"Damn straight." She reached down beside the couch and retrieved her purse to show him. "Peter gave it to me."

* * * *

Milonovich was about to climb into his car when his cellphone rang. He didn't recognize the number but answered anyhow.

"That you, Mr. Milonovich?" shouted Eugena Arquette. "You'll have to speak up."

"Call me George," he said. "What can I do for you, Mrs. Arquette?"

"You can call me Eugena," she said. "You're quite a handsome man, George, and I enjoyed our conversation the other day. I'd like to get to know you better, so I was wondering if you're available for dinner tomorrow evening."

He had no plans for the next evening and said so. "What are you suggesting?"

"My friends have raved about a steakhouse downtown. I was thinking we could try it out. If we order by five, we get the senior discount."

Milonovich had not dated much over the years, and though a few women of less-than-stellar reputation had propositioned him, he'd never been invited on a date because women of his generation didn't do that. His daughter had often told him he needed to adapt to the new world, and this was one change he thought he could live with. He said, "What time should I pick you up?"

* * * *

Milonovich had been at work for more than an hour before his daughter arrived. When she poked her head into his office to let him know she was in, he said, "You're late."

"Sorry. I didn't get to sleep until two a.m., and I had a hard time getting started this morning."

"After you've settled in, come see me. We need to discuss the Tucker case. It's driving me nuts."

She joined him a few minutes later, and he fired off his first question as soon as she settled into the chair on the far side of his desk. "Why didn't you tell me our client was blond?"

"Sandra's not a suspect."

"She certainly had a good reason to want Tucker dead. She inherited his stock, so now she's the majority shareholder, and her fingerprints are in his house."

"Her alibi is rock solid," Tonya said. "The night Tucker died, Sandra was at a party with several friends of mine, and she left with one of them."

"You confirmed this?"

"With every one of them," Tonya said.

"And the guy she left with? When did they part company?"

"Dianne swears Sandra didn't leave her apartment until just after sunrise. They both had to get to work that Friday morning."

"Then we're done," Milonovich told his daughter. "We'll have to tell Ms. Hellerman that we can't prove Peter Tucker's death was anything other than what it appears."

"And the woman seen leaving his home that evening?"

"A red herring," Milonovich said. "It's unlikely any of the women we've talked to visited Tucker's home that evening. Those without solid alibis don't fit the description."

"And you're certain Mrs. Arquette's description of the woman is accurate?"

"I don't think her eyesight could be much better," he said. He sat up straighter. "She thinks I'm handsome. She invited me to dinner tonight."

Tonya's eyebrows rose in surprise. "A date, at your age?"

"What's my age have to do with anything?" Milonovich asked. "The only date I'll ever turn down is the one with death."

Tonya shook her head. "Why don't you talk to Mrs. Arquette over dinner, see if her description of the woman she saw that night remains the same."

"I don't want to mix business with pleasure."

His daughter reminded Milonovich that without business, he would not have the opportunity for pleasure.

As she stood to leave, something on Tonya's left hand glittered, catching his attention. He stopped her and pointed. "What's that?"

"Dad," Tonya said as she thrust her left hand toward her father to show him her engagement ring, "I'm getting married."

Surprised, Milonovich said, "Who is he? Why haven't I met the guy?"

"It's Brenda."

"Your roommate?" There was an uncomfortable moment of silence until a look of realization slowly crossed Milonovich's face. "I'm not much of a detective, am I?"

"You don't see what you don't want to see," his daughter said. "You've always been that way."

"But—"

"There's no better time to ask this, but I want you at the wedding. I want you to give me away."

Milonovich swallowed hard. No matter what else she was, Tonya was his daughter. "I would be honored to."

* * * *

Milonovich arrived at Eugena's home precisely at four p.m. He wore his best suit again. She wore an evening dress and carried a Louis Vuitton bag.

He pointed to it and said, "That's how you recognized what the woman in red was wearing?"

"I'd be surprised if most of the women in this neighborhood don't have at least one Louis Vuitton," she told him.

He escorted her to his car, held the door while she slipped into the passenger seat, and then joined her. Soon, they were headed downtown.

"Have you closed your case yet?" Eugena asked. "Was Mr. Tucker murdered?"

"I may be getting too old to do this stuff," Milonovich said. "Looks as if it's just like the police said."

Eugena touched his arm. "You're never too old."

"I'm thinking it's time to step away from day-to-day operation of the business and let my daughter take over. She's been ready for a long time, and I just refuse to get out of her way."

"That's one of the reasons my son moved away. He said he could never be his own man as long as he lived near his father. I'm guessing you have a better relationship with your daughter."

"Not as close as I'd thought," he said. He told Eugena about his daughter's engagement to the woman he thought was her roommate, and how he would be walking his daughter down the aisle at her wedding. She didn't seem surprised.

By the time he finished, they had parked at The Cattle Baron's Club. The restaurant occupied a converted warehouse, and much of the building was given over to the affiliated nightclub, which featured live country music on the weekends and variety of shows and special events during the week that catered to the cultural diversity of the surrounding neighborhood.

They were shown directly to a table near the back, where they were seated near other older couples the restaurant had also hidden from view. Over dinner and a shared bottle of wine they continued the conversation they'd had in her kitchen before he'd questioned her about the night of Peter Tucker's death. They talked about their marriages, about their children, and about her grandchildren. They talked about how the world had changed, how their bodies had changed, and how dating was so much different at their age than it had been when they were young.

They stared into one another's eyes, laughed at each other's jokes, and Milonovich found himself drawn to Eugena in a way that he had not been drawn to a woman in a great many years.

As they exited The Cattle Baron's Club after dinner, Milonovich stopped at the entrance to the affiliated nightclub to examine a list of upcoming events. He was thinking of inviting Eugena out for a second date and hoped something he saw would provide a good reason for the invitation. Friday and Saturday evenings featured unfamiliar country bands, and Tuesday was Open Mic Comedy Night. Wednesday was Hump Day, with two-for-one specials all night, and Thursday had a rotating schedule of events. The first Thursday of each month featured a Drag Show.

Milonovich pointed it out to Eugena. "The world is falling apart."

She agreed with him. "It isn't like when we were growing up," she said. "Nowadays all the girls want to be boys and all the boys want to be girls."

He nodded his head in agreement and took her hand for the walk to his car. They didn't talk much during the drive back to Eugena's home, but at her front door, he leaned in for a kiss. She stretched up to meet it.

When the kiss ended, Eugena said, "Why don't you come in for a nightcap and I'll let you shout sweet nothings in my ear."

"That's a little forward."

"I'm too damn old to stand on ceremony," she said, "so let's not dither around. You coming in or not?"

He did.

* * * *

The next morning, Milonovich drove directly from Eugena's home to the office, where he found his daughter sitting at her computer typing a final report to their client.

"Save that and come with me," he said.

Once they were in his car, she asked, "Have you changed cologne?"

"I—"

"Are you wearing the same clothes you wore last night?" Then she answered her own question. "You are. You haven't been home yet, have you?"

"There wasn't time."

As they arrived at Sonny Tucker's home, she said, "You think Peter Tucker's ex-wife killed him? How do you figure it?"

"Follow my lead."

Milonovich leaned into the doorbell, and then pounded on the door when no one answered immediately.

The deceased's ex-wife finally pulled the door open and Milonovich pushed in past her. "We need to talk."

"Can't this wait? My son's already left for work."

"Which bedroom is his?"

"First one on the left at the top of the stairs, but—"

"Keep her busy," he instructed his daughter before he climbed the stairs.

Once inside Sonny's bedroom, he opened the closet and examined every piece of clothing. Then he opened every dresser drawer and tore through them, not finding what he had hoped to find.

He stopped, leaned against the wall, and took a deep breath.

"Dad," Tonya called up from the foyer. "What are you looking for?"

He moved on to Andrea's bedroom, where he found a Louis Vuitton leather purse wrapped in a plastic trash bag on the upper shelf of the closet. He made his way downstairs and showed his daughter the purse. "This. No woman is going to throw away a three-thousand-dollar purse just because it has a few bloodspots on it."

He turned to Andrea. "Where's the red dress?"

"I burned it."

"And the blond wig, the gloves?"

"I burned them, too."

Tonya was starting to catch the drift. "Does your son know what you did that night? Is he covering for you?"

Milonovich crossed the living room and grabbed one of the photographs from the mantle, one of Andrea standing with a younger blonde. He shoved it in her face, "Or are you covering for him?"

"I— I—" Andrea covered her face and sank onto the couch.

Tonya turned to her father. "Sonny killed his father?"

Milonovich nodded. Then he had his daughter phone Anna Kendrick, her friend in the Crime Scene Unit, about the purse he'd found. Kendrick arrived a little later with a pair of Homicide detectives in tow.

They weren't pleased to be there until Milonovich spelled everything out for them and Andrea confirmed his conclusions.

* * * *

On the way back to the office after giving statements to the police, Milonovich explained to his daughter. "Eugena and I didn't spend the entire night playing slap and tickle. She's pretty sharp with a computer."

He told his daughter that the first Thursday of every month The Cattle Baron's Club hosted a Drag Show, an evening for crossdressers. "Tucker had dinner with Nikki Wilson at The Cattle Baron's Club the night he died, and that same night was a first Thursday Drag Show. After we returned to her house, Eugena found The Cattle Baron's Club's website and we scoured every first Thursday photo until we found this."

He placed a computer-generated photoprint on the desk. "It's the same woman in the photos on the mantle at Sonny's home, and we were pretty sure none of the people in the photos on the club's website were female. That meant only one thing."

"Sonny's a crossdresser."

"But Sonny didn't just crossdress," Milonovich explained. "He dresses in his mother's clothes."

"What was the clincher?"

"Before I left her home this morning, Eugena used the computer again to show me pictures of the purse she'd seen the night of Tucker's death. When I found a match in Andrea's closet, I knew I was right. Sonny killed his father."

"But why?"

* * * *

They didn't learn the reason until several days later, after they pieced together what the dead man's ex-wife told them while awaiting the arrival of the police, what Tonya learned from her former lover in the Crime Scene Unit, and what they were able to glean from newspaper articles about Sonny's confession.

After Nikki Wilson dumped Peter Tucker the night she dined with him at The Cattle Baron's Club, she left him alone at the restaurant. Tucker finished his dinner, walked into the bar, switched from red wine to Scotch, and continued drinking. He was well into his cups when the transvestites starting showing up for that evening's Drag Show, and he hit on several of them, not realizing what they were under their clothing.

Sonny was there, too, wearing his mother's things. He'd been doing it since he was a teenager and had only done it in public after his mother left his father to move in with him. When Tucker hit on Sonny, clearly not recognizing his own son underneath the make-up, blond wig, and women's clothing, Sonny lowered his voice to a near-whisper and played along.

"You remind me of my wife," Tucker told him between drinks.

"Is she as beautiful as me?"

"She's a stone-cold bitch, but I'd do her again in a New York minute."

That bothered Sonny, but he held it together until Tucker downed so much Scotch he could barely keep himself upright. Then Sonny suggested they go to Tucker's place for a nightcap. Tucker, apparently thinking he was going to score, agreed.

Sonny drove, helped his father into the house, and settled him fully dressed onto his bed. By then, the alcohol had begun to wear off and Tucker opened his eyes. In the bright light he recognized his son and they argued—starting with how Sonny was dressed but mostly about Sonny's mother and how Tucker had treated her during all their years of marriage. When Tucker wouldn't stop, Sonny reached into the nightstand and pulled out Tucker's revolver.

With the revolver pressed against his temple, Tucker continued his tirade of insults. "You thumb-sucking, momma's skirt-hugging, candy ass. You don't have the guts to pull the trigger."

He was wrong.

Sonny had only a moment to think about what he'd done. He put the gun in his father's hand, hurried out of the house, and called for a cab to meet him several blocks away. He had the driver drop him off several blocks from The Cattle Baron's Club, where he'd left his car in the parking lot.

He drove home, told his mother what he'd done, and they burned the dress, gloves, wig, and other clothes Sonny had been wearing, destroying everything but the Louis Vuitton leather purse he'd been carrying that night.

After Sonny's confession, the insurance company paid off the key man policy, and, at Sandra Hellerman's suggestion, Milonovich and Daughter Private Investigators kept the unearned portion of the retainer Tucker Pucker Products had paid a few days earlier.

* * * *

Milonovich and his daughter were sitting in his office discussing a new client when an intern delivered a case of Tucker Pucker Products' bestselling product. He opened the box and pulled out what looked like a flashlight with a pair of lips where the lens should have been. Milonovich looked at his daughter. "What the hell is this?"

As Tonya explained what it was and how to use it, his face grew red.

Not just the city, Milonovich decided, but the entire world was turning into Sodom and Gomorrah.

Michael Bracken, recipient of the Edward D. Hoch Memorial Golden Derringer Award for lifetime achievement, is author of several books, including *All White Girls*, and more than 1,200 short stories published in *Alfred Hitchcock's Mystery Magazine*, *Ellery Queen's Mystery Magazine*, and many other publications. He lives and writes in Texas.

A DISTURBANCE IN THE HAREM
Elizabeth Zelvin

"Are you listening, old friend?" the administrative mistress of the harem snapped. "It is not like you to fall to daydreaming. I said, I need your help, and it is urgent!"

"I am sorry, Kethüda Hatun," the Kizlar Agha said. "Tell me how I may serve you."

Indeed, the whole *haremlik* was designed to be a daydream—if you were a silly slave girl imagining that you would win the Sultan's favor, bear his son, and at length become Valide Sultan, mother of a Sultan and most powerful woman in the Ottoman Empire, which was likely to swallow half of Europe if the current emperor, Suleiman, had his way. The perfumed baths, thick carpets, gauzy curtains, and jeweled and filigreed lanterns took hard work to maintain in a constant state of perfection: the work of an army of eunuchs under the command of the Kizlar Agha. It had not been his dream as a boy running free in the African forests, before his capture and castration. But it was his job.

The Kethüda Hatun handled the money: household expenses, the ladies' daily stipends, and the gifts in treasure and valuables that came pouring in for the royal princesses, sisters and daughters of the Sultan, who lived in the *haremlik* along with his concubines and their many attendants.

"Treasure is missing," the Kethüda Hatun said, "and it must be found before the viziers start asking questions. I do not want to end my days sewn into a sack with a load of rocks and thrown into the Bosphorus. I would not trouble you, but the Valide is in Manisa on state business. The new favorite, Hürrem, is not inclined to beg favors for anyone but herself. And her defeated rival, Mahidevran, when she is not sulking, is too busy doting on her son to be helpful. She still hopes the Sublime One's fondness for the boy will lead him to smile on her once more."

The Kizlar Agha snorted.

"I do not know which of them is more foolish. Mahidevran knows that no concubine may bear a second son. How else is fratricide to be avoided? And Hürrem boasts that she will so enchant the Sultan that he will break tradition and marry her."

"Someone had better drop a word in her ear, then," the Kethüda Hatun said, "about the penalties for witchcraft. Yet she is no fool. She calculated her stipend fast enough. And I heard her questioning the Jewish woman, Kira Rachel, about how she sets the price of the wares from the Bedestan that she purveys to the harem."

Gossip was the curse of the harem, but it served to distract the Kethüda Hatun, an intelligent woman herself. The Kizlar Agha had been gazing at one of the newer Palace eunuchs. The boy—Akisou, a Nubian name—was a beauty. He frowned, annoyed at himself for knowing the young slave's name. He must forget it. He had long ago vowed not to have favorites. It was bad for discipline, and without discipline, the harem would become a flock of screaming peacocks in a cage too small for them. The policy had served him well. Rising in the ranks of harem service to rule the whole *haremlik* under three sultans, he had learned to be content with fine clothes, exceptional jewels, the joy of reading the finest poets and philosophers in several languages, and the considerable pleasures of the table.

"I will look into this, *hatun*," he said. "We do not want the viziers interfering with the business of the harem."

* * * *

"The Kizlar Agha has commanded my presence," Rachel said. "Sammy, if you must chase the last dumpling around the soup, use the spoon, not your fingers."

"But, Mama, it's Shabbat." Her youngest cast a melting brown-eyed glance up at her through thick, straight black hair like that of his Taino father. "A spoon is a tool. If I use it, is it not work, which is forbidden?"

"He got his gift of argument from you, *nanichi*," Ümīt said. "If I'd had it, the rabbis would never have refused my petition to convert to Judaism. Which reminds me, young scamp, that like your papa, you are Muslim. So fingers out of the soup. What does he want, Rachel?"

"I do not know," Rachel said. "Spoons! How did we get so civilized?"

"You were always civilized, my love," he said. "As for me, blame it on Admiral Columbus."

"I do," she said. "He was kind to me, but I can never forgive what he did to the Taino."

"It does not bear thinking about, *nanichi*," Ümīt said. "Today we are blessed. When are you to see the Kizlar Agha?"

"Tomorrow morning," Rachel said.

"But it is Shabbat, Mama!" Little Sammy stuffed a date into his mouth and spoke around it, dodging a cuff on the ear from his older brother

Moshe, known as Musa at the *medrese* where he studied Qur'an.

"Do not attempt to chew and speak at the same time, my son," Ümīt said. "It limits your power to do either effectively."

"Unless you wish to become a muezzin," Moshe said, "calling the Faithful to prayer. Then it might be a useful vocal exercise."

"And you are Jewish, Mama, or you could not be a *kira*."

"If we had not learned to tolerate a great deal of inconsistency," Rachel said, "not a single Mendoza would have made it out of Spain alive back in 1492, much less reached Istanbul to prosper and produce such cheeky children."

* * * *

"I require your assistance," the Kizlar Agha said, "on a matter of accounting."

The *kira* raised shapely brows in inquiry.

"Are not such matters the province of the Kethüda Hatun?"

"They are," he said. "She has consulted me."

"And you in turn consult me," Rachel said, "because something valuable is missing."

"That is an excellent deduction," the Kizlar Agha said. "Tell me how you reached it."

"Certainly, *effendi*," she said. "Ordinarily, you do not involve yourself in the everyday affairs of the harem. I am a businesswoman. I deal daily with vendors in the Bedestan and customers in the harem. I know perfectly well that accounting is completely unremarkable—until the moment when something does not add up."

He nodded, a small egret feather held in place by a modest ruby brooch—one's turban must never outdo the Sultan's—dipping briefly.

"Have you made any further deductions?"

"I surmise that a search of the *haremlik* has revealed nothing."

"And now you wonder why I have involved you."

"That, *effendi*," she said, "I believe I know. Among the vast population of this place, I am the only female who passes freely between the *haremlik* and the outside world."

"Exactly. Except for you, only the Valide ever leaves this gilded honeycomb. And the Sultan's mother has no need to steal what she may take at will."

"You must believe I had opportunity for thievery," she said.

"Do you dispute it?"

"If you will tell me precisely what was taken and when," she said, "I may be able to prove I was elsewhere at the time."

"I do not have that information," he admitted.

"Then may I question the Kethüda Hatun? She would not have been worried enough to seek your help unless she had sufficient evidence to make outsiders look askance at her stewardship. The viziers and their auditors, perhaps?"

"She will be summoned."

"Do you also believe I had motive?" she asked. "I have everything I need: love, work, and family."

"Everyone wants riches," he said.

"Perhaps you do not know my history, *effendi*," Rachel said. "In my youth, I sailed to what is now called the New World with Admiral Columbus and my brother. I was offered the riches of that fabled place. The gold we found there came soaked in the blood of people I held dear, and I did not want it. I refused it. I will clear my name, and once I do, I will help you find your missing treasure."

* * * *

He would long since have died of boredom and despair, the Kizlar Agha reflected, if he had not found people interesting. On the *selamlik* side of the Palace, many were dangerous. It was that which made them interesting. On the *haremlik* side, few were interesting, but if they were, that made them dangerous. He could not remember the last time he had met someone who was interesting without being dangerous.

"What first brought the problem to your attention?" Kira Rachel asked the Kethüda Hatun. "The smallest detail may be important."

"It was Gülsen Hatun's pet monkey," the *hatun* said, with a nervous glance at the Kizlar Agha. "It dropped a gold ducat into my lap."

"I am acquainted with Gülsen Hatun's monkey." Rachel grinned. "Indeed, I acquired it for her in the Grand Bazaar at her insistence. It is excessively fond of bright, shiny objects. But why should Gülsen Hatun not have a gold ducat?"

"The *hatuns* receive a daily stipend in silver *akçe*," the Kethüda Hatun explained. "The more prudent ladies leave their funds with me to draw upon as needed. But Gülsen must have every silver coin put in her hand at once. When you lay out the contents of that great trunk of yours, have you ever known her *not* to purchase something that took her fancy?"

"No." Rachel laughed. "If she admires a length of brocaded silk from Cathay that matches her eyes, she must have it. And if she has not the full sum in hand, she begs me prettily, with tears, to give her credit."

"And do you extend her credit?" the Kizlar Agha asked.

"I have daughters, *effendi*," Rachel said. "I love them dearly, but I am not so easily moved by tears."

"Then we have something in common," he said. "Do you take the *hatun*'s point about the gold ducat, *kira*?"

"I do," she said. "When I consider her character, I agree she could not hold on to a hundred silver *akçe* long enough to exchange it for a single Venetian ducat—or even eighty for a Viennese ducat. I might say the same of one or two other spendthrift young *hatuns*."

The Kizlar Agha stroked his lips with two beautifully manicured fingers to hide a smile.

"You can distinguish each one of my flock of vain and silly peahens from the rest?"

"They are people!" Rachel said. "I spend much time conversing with them, and I have come to know their interests and desires. Gülsen may be frivolous, but she loves animals and treats them with patience and kindness, even that pesky monkey. Dilara is fond of the works of the poet Rumi."

"As am I," the Kizlar Agha murmured.

"Sevgi is partial to sad love stories. She cries over the tale of Leyla and Mecnun no matter how many times she hears it. Halime hates injustice and will stand up for a younger or weaker girl she sees being teased or bullied."

"You will spend even more time among them," he decreed. "They will confide in you. Even if only one of them is guilty of theft, others may have seen or heard something that means little to them, but may prove illuminating to us."

Over time, the theft amounted to a considerable sum in gold ducats. Records had been altered, which indicated that the thief had been both literate and numerate.

"What about Hürrem Hatun?" Rachel asked. "She is good with figures, and she is ambitious."

The Kizlar Agha snorted.

"All favorites are ambitious. I have seen them come and go. The Sultan beds them, they bear his son—or a daughter or two first, and then a son—then they become the mother of a prince and devote themselves to scheming for his accession, while the Sultan beds another girl and it starts all over again. Look at Mahidevran. This one will be just the same."

"I am not so sure," Rachel said. "I believe Hürrem's ambitions may be political."

"What! You had better tell me, girl, if the Sultan's bedmate contemplates treason."

"You mistake me, *effendi*," Rachel said. "I believe Hürrem wishes to model herself on the Valide Sultan and endear herself to the Sublime One by taking an interest in affairs of state. She dreams of a life at the Sultan's side and an influence beyond the confines of the *haremlik*."

"How do you know this?"

"She corresponds with the Venetian ambassador—merely a cordial social exchange, I assure you: she swore at the start that she would not say a word concerning policy. I not only carry her letters, I act as her translator and scribe, as she knows no Italian. She asked me many questions about him before she ventured to approach him."

The Kizlar Agha's eyebrows shot up so high that he could feel them tickle the edge of his turban.

"You know the Venetian ambassador?"

"Yes, I am acquainted with all the European diplomats in Istanbul." She sounded quite composed. "Between my brother's business ventures and my husband's duties—you know he serves the Sultan—we have many social connections. I assure you, the Venetian ambassador is quite as fascinated with Hürrem Hatun as she is with him. He calls her Roxelana and raves about her beauty."

"Which he will never see," the Kizlar Agha said.

"He seems to require no fuel for his imagination," Rachel said.

"Christian fool," the Kizlar Agha said. "Suleiman will take Europe—Venice by sea, Vienna by land—and we will have all their ducats."

"And Hürrem?"

"You will read all her letters," he said, "as well as those she receives from Venice and any other friends she makes outside these walls."

"What about Mahidevran?" Rachel asked. "She has had a mighty fall. She was the Sultan's favorite for a long time while he governed Manisa, and after his accession her son was the heir apparent. Might she not seek consolation? Or revenge?"

"I do not know if Mahidevran has the wit for such a scheme," he said. "She is brighter than the rest, or she would not have held Suleiman's attention for so long. The Valide did not want to make that mistake again. That is why she brought in this current batch of pretty nitwits. Hürrem was clever enough to slip past her."

It became harder by the minute to guard his tongue around this bright-eyed Jewish woman. He found he did not care. Her whole being shone with integrity like the beacon of the Kiz Kulesi guiding ships to shore. It gave him pleasure to be himself with her—within reason.

"Mahidevran is more of a sulker than a plotter," he said, "and in her livelier moments, a scratcher and a hair puller. We shall see."

"There is another," Rachel said, "who *could* pass from *haremlik* to *selamlik* and back with impunity."

"Ha! You mean the monkey." The Kizlar Agha laughed aloud.

"It would not have acted alone," she said, lips twitching. "Perhaps the chief criminal is a well-educated man who resides elsewhere."

"A clever man with the monkey as accomplice? No," he said, "the harem must be involved. The accounts could only be tampered with from within. If the monkey had escaped to the *selamlik* even once, I doubt it would have returned, or indeed, survived—trampled by a janissary's horse or eaten by a hunting leopard, more likely."

"What about a janissary as the criminal? They are extremely well educated."

"They are indeed. The Enderun is the best school in the world. In the Palace School, the janissaries learn mathematics, navigation, astronomy, equitation, archery, swordcraft, engineering, languages, administration, music, calligraphy, philosophy, poetry, law, Qur'an—and that is not the whole curriculum. But a janissary who set foot in the harem would not live to tell the tale."

In his youth, before he had decided that he must choose between suicide and leaving bitterness behind, the Kizlar Agha had spent much time comparing the fate of the boys of the *devşirme*—the Christian tribute boys from Serbia and Albania who were converted to Islam and raised in the Enderun School, to rise in time to be the Sultan's generals, his admirals, his viziers, and his sons-in-law—and the African boys who were captured, mutilated, and then buried in sand up to their necks, to die of their wounds within three days or to live and be sold into a life of slavery, however luxurious that slavery, in his case, had turned out to be.

There were white eunuchs, too. Those destined for the Palace were less drastically cut than the black eunuchs and served in the *selamlik* under the Kapi Agha. The Qur'an forbade that a Muslim be enslaved or neutered. Once they were enrolled in the *devşirme* and converted, they were safe. So a Christian boy who was caught by slavers rather than by the Sultan's tribute collectors was simply phenomenally unlucky.

"Are we certain," Rachel asked, "that the gold has left the harem?"

She picked up a glass in a filigree holder from the small gilded table that lay between them and took a sip of thick, sweet mint tea.

"It must have," the Kizlar Agha said, "first to the *selamlik*, and thence, we must assume, to the outside world. A thorough search has been made. The falsified amounts are no longer within these walls."

"I did not take it," she said, "nor did the monkey. The women do not leave the harem. Who is left?"

"You wish me to say it must have been one of the eunuchs."

He drummed his fingers on the table, making the remaining glass and the finely worked bronze teapot jump and clatter.

"Four hundred sixty-seven eunuchs currently serve the *haremlik*. I would have said that all are loyal—more, devoted to me personally, a devotion that is flawed only in comparison to our common devotion to the Sultan. Am I to put every one of them to the question?"

She regarded him with sympathy in her dark eyes. Sympathy! He could not remember anyone giving him such a look since he had left his mother's house to hunt antelope in the forest all those years ago.

"It is worrisome. But setting that aside for now, what is even more portable than gold?"

The woman read him far too easily. She realized he would rather bend his mind to a conundrum than ward off feelings of which no one else dreamed he was capable.

"You mean jewels."

"Gemstones or jewelry, worked pieces."

"The Kethüda Hatun did not mention missing jewels."

"We did not ask her," Rachel said. "One does get so excited when gold is mentioned. I had ample opportunity to observe *that* phenomenon among Admiral Columbus's men."

The Kizlar Agha rose and shook out his robes, feeling unaccountably more cheerful.

* * * *

Mending a tear in Hatice Hatun's *salvar* with stitches so tiny as to be almost invisible, Rachel listened to the ladies' prattle while maintaining the appearance of being completely absorbed in drawing the silken thread through the baggy trousers, thin as gossamer and embroidered with seed pearls. Sewing was not her favorite task, but Hatice swore she had more skill than any of the harem seamstresses. She did not like spying, but she enjoyed the company of the *hatuns*. "Do you not pity them?" her sisters occasionally asked. "No more than I pity hens roosting in a henhouse," she would say. And emitting much the same sort of clamorous cackle, she thought now.

"I think Sevgi has a lover," Gülsen said. "She has the same look about her eyes that my little cat Esmer did after she got out into the *selamlik*, and two months later she had kittens."

"I do not!" Sevgi said.

"Look, girls, she is blushing," Halime said. "Well, it is not one of us, or two of us would have the look."

"Maybe it is a eunuch," Dilara said.

The remark elicited a general outcry.

"That is forbidden!"

"They have not the equipment!"

"Zerdali, you say that, who have toyed with every maidservant in the place? All they need is a mouth, a pair of hands, and an imagination."

Gülsen made a show of putting her hands over the youngest *hatun*'s ears.

"Do not listen, Elmas. Time enough for that kind of talk when you have been summoned to the Bedchamber."

"Elmas is not interested. She is too fond of honeyed sweetmeats to care about the pleasures of love. Have you not noticed how plump she is becoming?"

"*I* was summoned. Would you like to see my necklace?"

"We have all seen your necklace, Aysun. And you were summoned *once*, when Mahidevran had a fever and before the Merry One appeared to take up all His attention."

"I would like very much to see your necklace, Aysun," Rachel said.

She rose, wincing as her knees cracked. Once she had run up the rigging of Admiral Columbus's flagship as nimbly as any boy.

She must look closely at Aysun's necklace. A bedgift from the Sultan was no small thing. Rachel had handled many gems since becoming a purveyor to the harem, but she was no expert, to tell the priceless from the flawed. Perhaps some of the magnificent pendants, rings, and brooches in the storehouse were not the treasures that they seemed, but copies. Or the gems set in the originals might have been replaced by inferior stones.

* * * *

"A master jeweler of the highest probity must be brought in to see if anything has been replaced, *effendi*," she urged the Kizlar Agha. "Even one or two large pieces would make for a much more efficient theft than smuggling out gold ducats a few at a time."

"It would be a much more logistically complex theft," he said. "First, the thieves would have to find a master forger. None would dare approach one of the Palace artisans to execute such a forgery. Their whole lives are here, and they are well rewarded and fiercely loyal."

"The best craftsmen outside the Palace are found in the Bedestan," Rachel said. "I know several in the covered market, though I am not acquainted with any forgers."

"They would be the same," the Kizlar Agha said. "A master craftsman skilled enough to do the work and bribed well enough to swear silence, or better, thoroughly intimidated. No woman could inspire such fear, even if she could leave the harem."

"You favor a eunuch, then," Rachel said, "or a conspiracy between a woman and a eunuch. Need the woman be a *hatun*? What about a bath attendant, a seamstress, or a laundress? The Sultan's ladies come from faraway lands. They have no families to support, and they are given everything they desire. But might not an attendant have a family in the city whom she wished to help?"

"A *fakir* family in need of a pasha's ransom?"

"Let us first find out if there have been substitutions," she said. "Can we perhaps show any suspect pieces to one of the Palace artisans? That could be done in the *selamlik*, discreetly, of course."

"If it becomes known outside the *haremlik* that there are questions regarding the treasury," the Kizlar Agha said, "we risk the Kethüda Hatun's reputation and mine, the very thing I hope to avoid. Do you think me cowardly?"

"Not at all!" Rachel said. "Your duty is to preserve the peace of the *haremlik* above all. In Hebrew, we call it *shalom bayit*—the peace of the home. Well, it means marital harmony. But the harem really is one big marriage—not just the Sultan and the *hatuns*, but the whole thing, isn't it? And you *are* trying to preserve it."

"The Greeks of old would have called your argument sophistry. But I thank you. Which master jeweler in the Bedestan would you recommend, then, for both expertise and integrity?"

"My favorites are not jewelers," she said, "but a family of swordmakers. They work with gems and precious metals as well as steel, and they can make sword hilts as intricate as any necklace or tiara. Do you remember a great jeweled sword that Sultan Selim had, a gift from his mother while he was still a prince? It was my first big commission when I became a *kira*. Ayşe Hatun said it must be perfect. I was scared to death of her."

The Kizlar Agha chuckled.

"So was I."

"Of course I sought out the best swordmaker in the Bedestan. Mustafa and I became great friends. He is dead now, but I still do business with his sons and grandsons, fine craftsmen all."

"A family business. Good. If they have set out their trunks in the Bedestan for generations, they will know exactly which members of their craft are known for villainy."

"I will ask them if I must. They are good men, and we are very fond of one another."

"Fond! Young Gülsen is fond of that monkey. Can they be trusted? I require absolute discretion in this matter!"

"They are completely trustworthy," she said. "If they give me their word, they will keep it."

"I am not accustomed," the Kizlar Agha said, sounding more than he cared to like the Valide Sultan, the haughtiest person he knew, "to take the bare word of a vendor in the market."

"They must not be harmed in any way! If you will not give me your oath on that, I will not ask them."

The *kira*'s jaw set in a way that reminded the Kizlar Agha how little time he spent with women who were not schooled to compliance.

"Very well," he said. "You have my word. We must still find someone to identify any inferior pieces in the treasury."

"My friends can—oh! they cannot enter the harem."

"Not unless you wish me to castrate them first," he said, "and kill them afterwards. As I believe I have just promised not to do."

* * * *

Fortunately, the swordmakers were able to propose a happier solution. Rachel remembered Mustafa's grandfather as an elderly man who had relinquished the running of the business to his sons and retired to grow olives on a small farm on the outskirts of the city. It appeared that he was still alive. At the age of 105, he had outlived his wives and children but still took a lively interest in the affairs of his descendants.

"He rides into the city once a month on his favorite mule," the current head of the family told Rachel, "turns the household upside down de-manding that our wives cook all his favorite dishes, and pokes his fingers into every part of the business to make sure we aren't running it into the ground. If I may speak frankly, *kira*, grandpa is no threat to any woman. His parts shriveled twenty years ago. But his eyesight is still remarkably keen for his age, and he has worked with gems his whole life. If there is a single garnet posing as a ruby, he will know it."

Rachel duly reported all this to the Kizlar Agha.

"It is irregular," the Kizlar Agha said. "But we must know. I will allow it. His eyes must be tightly bound. I will send an escort of armed eunuchs—*mute* armed eunuchs. Do not look at me that way, Kira Rachel. It is sometimes done by slavers before they come under our protection. And he must come when the whole harem is sleeping."

"It had better be done soon," Rachel said. "Supposing valuable pieces *are* missing, every day's delay makes it more likely that they have been broken up."

"I agree," he said. "If the gems are already on their way to Antwerp or Cathay, we are undone. The visit will take place tonight. You have done your part, *kira*, and I am grateful."

* * * *

Rachel felt great eagerness to arrive at work the following morning. There was no way to enter the Sultan's Palace in a hurry. A great crowd always had business there, and the janissaries guarding the outermost gate moved at a magisterial pace. At the Gate of Salutation, a double escort of eunuchs appeared: some to carry her trunks to the harem, the rest to escort her directly to the Kizlar Agha's apartments.

There was no hurrying the Kizlar Agha either. First she must be made comfortable on a mountain of luxurious cushions opposite his own. Then the thick, sweet mint tea must be poured and sweetmeats offered. Rachel had eaten nothing at home in her haste to be gone, so she accepted a sticky pastry, bolted it, and licked her fingers.

"Do not toy with me, *effendi*. What have you found?"

The Kizlar Agha had the gilded table cleared and laid on it a bundle wrapped in crimson velvet cloth.

"Open it."

Rachel unwrapped the folds with trembling fingers, revealing a massive silver brooch set with an intricate pattern of diamonds, rubies, and emeralds.

"It was a gift from Mehmet the Conqueror," the Kizlar Agha said, "he who took Istanbul from the Byzantines, to Gülbahar Hatun, the mother of his son, Sultan Bayezid the Just, whom you remember."

"I do," Rachel said. "He welcomed the Jews to Istanbul when the kings of Spain and Portugal cast us out. It is magnificent. Is it not real?"

"The ancient gem master swore both stones and setting are false," the Kizlar Agha said. "He declared some of the gems outright counterfeit, some of inferior quality but cunningly set so that it would not be apparent. Furthermore, he read the forger's name in the workmanship as easily as I might read a verse of Rumi's poetry in Persian. The man will have been taken by now. We will have word as soon as he enters the Palace."

At that moment, an attendant entered and bent to whisper in the Chief Eunuch's ear.

"We are thwarted!" The Kizlar Agha banged the table with a clenched fist. "The man has hanged himself."

"My friends told no one!" Rachel said.

"I do not accuse them," the Kizlar Agha said. "Someone saw something, and that was enough. Rumor spreads like seed on the wind in the bazaar as it does in the Palace."

"Can we not simply leave the false brooch in the treasury?" Rachel asked. "If it has been there since the reign of Mehmet, who would notice?"

"Ordinarily, no one. But the current *haseki*, in addition to politics, has expressed an interest in history."

"I see," Rachel said. "The jewelry of past *hatuns*, which Hürrem Hatun would so love to hold in her hands, being part of that history. And what a pity to leave it lying about gathering dust."

"So our only remaining course is to catch the thief—or thieves," the Kizlar Agha said. "If the true brooch still exists, they still have it or know where it is. We must lull them into a false sense of security, then tempt them to put it back."

* * * *

The Kizlar Agha waited in the shadows, his eyes fixed on the treasury door, left cracked as if by chance. As if anything were ever left to chance in the household of Suleiman the Magnificent! His elite guard of mute eunuchs were but a shadow of a whisper looming on either side. Only a fool would expect forgiveness for the return of the Conqueror's brooch. But the world was full of fools.

"People believe what they want to believe," he had told the *kira* when she expressed incredulity that any slave of the Empire, having so transgressed, would imagine for a moment that he or she would be allowed to go free. "Having found gold ducats easy to dispose of, perhaps they were dismayed to find the jewels quite another matter. If they have grown desperate, the bargain we offer, however unlikely, may seem to them the only path to salvation."

He was wondering if his offer of amnesty had prompted his prey to bolt rather than spring the trap, when several things happened at once. Lanterns flared, the black robes of the guard swirled as they leaped, light glinted as it glanced off steel. The thieves, man and woman, were easily subdued.

"Bind them," he commanded. "Let us see whom we have caught."

If the female were no more than a humble attendant, he could dispose of her without fuss. But it was young Sevgi Hatun, tousled, red-faced, and defiant, from whom the eunuchs stripped veil and outer cloak.

"The plan was entirely mine!" she said. "Let Akisou go! I importuned him. He could not disobey a *hatun*."

Akisou. The Nubian eunuch. The Kizlar Agha felt sick. But he had not reached his present position by wearing his feelings on his face.

"Indeed? Akisou, remind me whose slave you are."

Akisou hung his head. Sweat ran down his forehead. An ashen pallor lay like grave dust on his copper-brown skin.

"I am the slave of the Sultan of Sultans, Sovereign of the Sublime House of Osman, and Commander of the Faithful."

"Bind them more securely and bring them where we may question them properly."

"But you said you would let us go if we returned the brooch!" Sevgi protested.

The Kizlar Agha gestured for both prisoners to be gagged. It would be a long night.

* * * *

"You are not drinking your mint tea, Kira Rachel. A pastry, perhaps?"

"Thank you, *effendi*, but I am not in the mood for sweets."

"You need not hear more," he said, "if you prefer."

"We set out to find the truth," she said. "I must not falter because I do not like the truth we have found. What will happen to Sevgi?"

"She must die. She stole from the Sultan. That cannot be tolerated."

"How?" she asked.

"A concubine who betrays the Sultan is cast into the Bosphorus."

"What was she thinking?" Rachel cried. "Sevgi was an innocent. Why?"

"Love, of course." The Kizlar Agha's tone was laced with mockery.

"Poor Sevgi," Rachel said. "Was the eunuch worthy?"

The Kizlar Agha shrugged.

"A pretty face. She saw him every day."

"I suppose they planned to run away together, like lovers in a tale."

"The woman begged to let them be sewn in the sack together, that they might face death in one another's arms."

"Will it be allowed?" she asked.

"It will not," he said.

Discreet though the *kira* was, he did not tell her that Akisou had not wished to face death in the *hatun*'s company. Under torture, he had admitted that the gold ducats she had believed would finance their flight had gone toward funding a rebellion of the Serbs against the Empire.

It was quite a romantic story, really. Akisou and the Serbian janissary Duşan ought never to have met. Duşan, heading back to barracks one night after smoking a potent mixture of opium and hemp with his mates, had strayed too near the harem precincts. Akisou had saved his life by stopping him. One didn't expect a boy of the *devşirme* to emerge from all those years of janissary training still a Serbian patriot. But it had happened. Duşan's passion was the Serbian cause, and Akisou's was Duşan. Akisou had begged to be sewn into the sack with Duşan. But the janissary's own commanders would execute him by the sword as a traitor to the Empire. The Sultan would have to be told. What a mess.

Nor would Kira Rachel ever learn the manner of Akisou's death. The Kizlar Agha had wielded the silken bowstring himself, weeping. A lowly slave was unworthy of such a death. But in the *haremlik*, the Kizlar Agha's word was law.

✗

Elizabeth Zelvin's stories have appeared in *Ellery Queen's* and *Alfred Hitchcock's Mystery Magazines* and been nominated twice for the Derringer and three times for the Agatha Award. Her historical novels in the Mendoza Family Saga are *Voyage of Strangers* and *Journey of Strangers*. She also writes the Bruce Kohler Mysteries.

SHOUT OUT TO ART TAYLOR!

In April, 2015 BK Stevens debuted the blog series, "The First Two Pages," in which writers talk about the craft of writing and analyze the first two pages of a published story. Art Taylor is now hosting the blog (including old entries) and continuing the series. We are delighted to have had a number of *Black Cat* stories featured, including "Crazy Cat Lady," by Barb Goffman, "Dixie Quickies," by Michael Bracken, and "Getting Away," by Alan Orloff. Check it out—it's fascinating stuff!

You can read the blog series here:

http://www.arttaylorwriter.com/blog-2/

(Due to the volume of posts, you may have to go through several pages to find the *Black Cat* entries.)

A WEIGHTY MATTER
Debra H. Goldstein

"Being dead leaves a lot to be desired. Killing someone is much more satisfying."

"Pardon?"

"Satisfying and pretty lucrative." He pulled a white handkerchief from his pocket and dabbed his bald head. "Being at your spa doesn't work for me."

The doctor, seated in a chair across from his, peered over her steel-framed readers at him. "Why is that?"

"Doc, look at the guests you have here. They're beautiful people. Toned, bronzed bodies, mini-bikinis, and six packs I can't believe. Are you going to tell me I'm not a fish out of water here?"

She made a note on the legal pad in her lap. "What makes you think that? Everyone who visits Haven Ranch and Spa fits in."

"Not me. I'm out of my element. A good hit man or woman blends with the crowd." He glanced out her picture window while again running his handkerchief over his forehead before returning it to his pants pocket.

"Are you telling me...?"

"Nah." He focused his gaze and grin back on her. "But I've always thought of it as an equal opportunity profession. Remember *The Sting*? I think that movie was right on the money."

She settled back in her chair, ankles crossed, pen poised. "I do remember being surprised when the assassin turned out to be a woman. But we were talking about you rather than movies."

"I like movies. I believe everyone can find something in them they can use in their lives. Don't you?"

"Maybe, but in my profession, we prefer to talk in terms of reality rather than imagination."

"Well, movies can influence reality. Think of a good hit."

"I'd rather not."

"Come on, follow me here. If I was doing a hypothetical hit, I wouldn't want to do it in an alley or out of the way. My trademark would be using a public place."

She leaned forward. "But that would make it more dangerous. You'd have a better chance of getting caught."

"Maybe, but once I got close to my mark, I wouldn't mess around. I'd do my job and leave."

"And you think you could consistently get away with killing someone in a place where there are lots of people?" Her brown hair gently rubbed against her shoulders as she shook her head. "I can't believe someone wouldn't stop you, or at least chase after you."

"Not if I did the hit with the same type of distraction a magician uses." He waved his hands in the air.

"I don't understand."

He laughed. "That's because you limit yourself to reality. I mix reality with imagination and trickery, so people aren't sure what they saw. I might leave the weapon stuck in the victim and keep walking. Or if I use a gun, let it fall from my fingertips into the first sewer or trashcan I pass. I'm not like that baseball player, the one who wore a green and gold uniform, whose satisfaction came from watching his hit zoom over the outfield wall. Nope, I think you do the job and let the scene fade to black."

"Sounds like you could write a movie." She tapped her pad. "Let's get back to why you're here. What seems to be the problems that brought you to see me today?"

"Bless your heart. I already told you why I scheduled a private session. This place is a challenge for me."

She uncrossed her legs. "I don't think I understand. All our guests are treated equally. The rooms are identical, the menus set, and everyone has access to the same trainers and exercise classes. Why do you feel different?"

"It's my weight. I could tell you I have a slow metabolism, but that would be a lie. I'm obsessed with food. Doesn't matter what kind. Don't just nod. I'm paying you for your words of wisdom. You like pizza? How much do you eat at one time?"

She rested the hand without a pen on her chin. "A piece or two, depending upon the toppings."

"I should have guessed that. You're an itty-bitty thing. I doubt you'd last in my business. You're almost too small to blend into a crowd. People would notice you because you're skin and bones and think you're an… an.… Help me here, what's the word?"

"Anorexic."

"That's it. Anorexic. Nobody will ever use that word for me," he said, patting his stomach. "I'd eat the slices you left behind and another small pizza for good measure."

"I don't believe that."

"Maybe I'm exaggerating a bit, but you get the idea."

"I'm not sure I do."

"Then let me give you another example." He pulled a shiny object from the pocket of his sports coat.

She stared at his hand.

"Relax. You ever cut open an avocado with a knife like this one? No?" He moved his hand so she could get a better view of the knife's short blade.

"It works well on an avocado. See, I hold the avocado up with this hand while I use the other to slice it lengthwise with one stroke. Then I pop the pit out with the knife's tip. Without the pit, it's smooth sailing to get the pulp out. A ripe avocado goes down easy and it's good for you. Problem is, I don't stop with just one."

"Sounds like your problem is related to portion control."

"That's what they've always told me. Weight Watchers, Jenny Craig, Medifast, and who knows what else. I've tried them all. The lifetime member pins I've accumulated over the years document my weight loss success. In fact, by my calculation, as well as the pictures in my photo albums, I've gained and lost at least three people during my lifetime."

He chuckled, but cut his laugh off by tightening his jaw. "These days, I'm up a person."

"I'm confused. You said those programs worked for you in the past. If you're miserable, why not use one of them again? There must be one you prefer."

"That's what I like about you, Doc. Your simple answers make problems seem simple."

Dropping her pen on her notepad, she leaned forward. "Am I missing something?"

"Nah, I'm messing with you." He paused and waited for her to sit back in her chair. "In my work, I pride myself on transforming into whatever part I play. I even charge my customers more for doing it."

She consulted her pad. "You didn't fill in your occupation, but I think I understand. You're like most of the other actors who come here. Conscious fluctuation of your weight is necessary for your work."

"Right. It's important to never look the same from job to job and to mix in easily. Knowing I was coming to a place like this, I did my homework and lost a part of me before I got here. It just wasn't enough to blend in with your crowd."

He hesitated, pressing his lips together.

She waited for him to continue.

"Losing weight for a job is getting harder. I guess it's my age. Take a guess. How old do you think I am?"

"I don't think I should."

"It's okay."

"No." She lowered her eyes and added another paragraph to her page of notes.

"Doc, I told you. Tell me how old you think I am."

Raising her head, she turned her eyes toward the windowed wall from which one could see a mountain ridge rising beyond the pool.

"Fifty."

"You're playing with me."

"I'm not." She met his gaze again.

"Either you're a lousy liar or you need new glasses. The fat hides my wrinkles, but let me lose a few pounds and my face looks like a shriveled prune topped with a gray film. Here, look at my arm. When I lose weight, the skin hangs. I don't remember who, but someone told me age makes it lose its elasticity."

She nodded.

"So, you were being polite? Or politically correct?"

"No. It was an honest guess."

"If you must tell me you're being honest, it makes me wonder. That doesn't bode well for me to trust you."

"Trust takes time to build. In the meantime, my job isn't to be polite. It's to help you identify your issues, even if it means asking hard questions. Once I know the underlying problems you're dealing with, I can be a safe sounding board while you figure out viable solutions."

"That sounds like a lot of mumble jumble. Maybe I went into the wrong profession."

She stole a peek at the clock on the wall. "Our time is almost up and I'm still not sure what's bothering you. Memories from your job intruding into your dreams or…"

"Nah, once I do a job, I'm done with it. And for your information, I'm sixty-five. Don't know where time's gone, but I'm ready to let younger folks take my place. You know how people talk about wanting a house with a white picket fence and a garden to putter in? I don't want that house. I want a no-maintenance condo in Florida where the real me can walk on the beach or sit and stare at the water."

"I'm not a real estate agent, but maybe in our next session we can talk about that condo and how you see yourself in it." She placed her pad on the side table.

"That's okay, Doc. The term is visualization. And well, it's simple math for me. One last score equals my vision becoming reality. I know

I'm going to have to lose weight using one of those diets we discussed, but at this point in my life, I'm not going to worry about whether I lose all of it. I'm going to let my body be whatever size it wants."

"Still, it helps to be a healthy weight. In addition to our counseling sessions, you might enjoy trying some of our weight loss and exercise classes."

"From what I've seen, you have a nice clinic and spa deal going here, but I don't think I'll be around long enough to take advantage of everything you offer. You see, not everyone is pleased with your treatment results. I wouldn't reach for that button if I were you. I wiped the blade off, but I hope you don't mind the taste of avocado."

✗

Judge Debra H. Goldstein is the author of the upcoming Sarah Blair series (Kensington), *Should Have Played Poker* and *Maze in Blue*. Her short stories appear in periodicals and anthologies, including *Alfred Hitchcock's Mystery Magazine*, *Mystery Weekly*, and *Day of the Dark*. She is a Sisters in Crime and SEMWA board member.

✗

COMING NEXT ISSUE!

SUBURBIA, by Michael Bracken

WHALE WATCH, by Charles Roland

THE SORORITY HOUSE, by Eve Fisher

DIVERSIONS, by John M. Floyd

TOURIST SEASON, by JM Taylor

THE LIST, by Charlie Drees

BEYOND A REASONABLE DOUBT, by Ashley Lynch-Harris

SOMETHING CERTAIN, by Peter W.J. Hayes

THE TARGET, by Charlie Hughes

THE MOMENT OF RIGHTING, by Robb T. White

Subscribe at bcmystery.com or wildsidepress.com

BURIED SECRETS
Steve Shrott

"I know what you did."

I turned to the blonde with the full lips and short black dress sitting beside me at the bar. "I'm sorry?"

"I saw you."

"Saw me do what, exactly?"

"You know."

I shook my head. "I'm afraid I don't. I've just been sitting here drinking."

She shrugged. "Okay, if that's the way you want to play it." She tapped her straw on the ice at the bottom of her glass.

I signaled to John the bartender to pass me another Guinness. John runs the bar here at the Comfort Inn Motel. He's a red-haired Irishman with a beer gut and some anger issues. But all in all, a good guy.

I thought I was finished with the blonde, but a moment later, she spoke again. "The body, for Christ's sake. The dead body."

My eyes snapped open. "What dead body?"

"The one you buried."

I stared at her, shocked.

She sipped her drink, then wiped her mouth as though it were a rare piece of art.

"Listen lady, I don't know who you think I am. But I'm not in the habit of burying dead bodies."

"I have pictures."

I crinkled my brow. "You couldn't possibly have pictures."

"I'll show you." She reached into her purse, tossing many objects around. "I must have left my phone up in the room."

I nodded. "I'm sure you did."

She ignored my comment, just looked at me with her big blue eyes. "Why don't we go and sit on one of those comfortable couches in the corner and talk a little more privately."

I didn't budge. "Nothing to talk about. You obviously have the wrong man."

She stood up, grabbed my hand. "Come on. It'll be fun."

My first inclination was to remove my hand from hers and leave. But she had me curious. Besides, she was nice to look at, and I really had nowhere else to go.

I followed her to a dark corner of the bar where she plopped down onto a leather couch. I sat next to her, a little distance away. A small fixture hung down from the ceiling, but the area was still dark. Shadows played across her face, making her look a bit like some kind of demon. Maybe she was. I swallowed more of my beer, then asked her name.

"Desiree."

"Nice."

"I like it." She giggled like a little girl who has just been told she's pretty. "And you?"

"Matt. Where are you fro—"

"Don't you want to know how I saw you?"

"You mean bury the body?"

"Uh huh."

I took a deep breath. "Sure, why not."

"Well, I was driving on Vine Street and stopped at a light. You were in the car next to me. You looked kinda cute and I waved to you. But you didn't wave back. I figured you were tense, having a body in the trunk and all. Then—"

"Hold it. I gotta stop you there. Your story is flawed."

"How is that?"

"You said the first time you saw me was when I stopped at the light. How could you know about anything in the trunk?"

She drank some of her Tom Collins, probably to give herself a chance to think. "Well, I didn't know that at the time. I'm just saying now that's probably why you were tense. Anyhow, as you drove off, I noticed that your car seemed to be leaking something—oil maybe, I don't know. I don't really know much about cars. But I figured I had to tell you."

"So you followed me, huh?"

"It seemed like the right thing to do. I was worried that something might happen to your car. So I drove behind you and went down the same streets you did. Eventually, I saw you stop near the place with all that forest area—the Verna...Verna..."

"The Vernasky Trail?"

"Right. I parked and was about to tell you about the oil thing when you walked into the forest. I followed and saw you do something strange. You felt the ground in several areas, grabbed some of the dirt. You had this terrible scowl on your face. I was suspicious about what you were doing, and a little frightened too. So I hid behind an oak tree and—"

I couldn't help but smirk. "You saw me feel the ground?"

"Yeah."

"Why would any sane person feel the ground?"

"It's obvious. You were seeing if it was soft enough to dig."

I sipped my drink then locked eyes with her. "I'm afraid there's a little something that disproves your whole story, honey. You said you were behind an oak tree. But there are no oak trees on the Vernasky Trail. Just maples. I worked for an arborist when I was young and know a lot about vegetation. The leaves of an oak never grow side by side. Maple leaves, on the other hand, grow in pairs, one on each side of the branch. Now, the mulberry—"

"Fine, fine. I was behind a maple tree. Doesn't matter." She stared at me a moment, then got this weird smile on her face as if she'd bested me in a game of pool. "I just thought of something. How could you know there aren't any oaks if you weren't there?"

I spread my hands. "Of course I've been there. It's a shortcut to the Morrison Cemetery where my grandmother is buried. She and I were very close, and I go and talk to her at the grave every few months."

"Whatever you say." She looked away for a moment, focusing on something in the distance, then turned back to me. "Anyhow, I stood behind the tree, and saw you open the trunk of your car and pull out a green garbage bag." She leaned toward me and whispered. "The size and shape of a body."

I studied her for a moment. "So you didn't really see the body."

"Actually, I did. When you dropped it and part of the bag ripped open, I saw his face."

"Okay, so what color was the hair?"

"I don't know. Couldn't make it out."

"Let me get this straight. You were a couple of yards away, and you couldn't make out the hair color. That sounds dubious."

She pouted. "I didn't want to make any noise reaching into my pocket to get my glasses."

I started to laugh. This was too much. But you know, it was kind of fun talking to her, and with all the stress I'd been under lately, I needed some fun. So I ordered another round for both of us. "Okay, I'm intrigued. What happened next?"

"You took out a shovel from your car and started digging. It took a while and you seemed to be getting pretty tired."

"Sure, I can see how I'd be tired after digging."

"You being sarcastic?"

"No, no. Just saying. It's natural I'd be tired after digging a hole for a dead body. Who wouldn't?"

She rolled her eyes. "Anyhow, I guess that's where you got that dirt on your pants." She pointed to the small mud stain on the front of my trousers.

I looked at her a moment, then at my pants. There was definitely dirt there.

"Got ya. That's one thing you can't deny."

"No, guess I can't." I drank a little of my beer, thinking.

She leaned forward and glared at me. "So why'd you do it?"

Instead of giving this lady a piece of my mind, I decided to call John over to our table. A few moments later, he stood in front of me.

"John, this lady asked me about the dirt here on my pants." I pointed to the stain.

"What about it?"

I didn't want to go into the whole story with him. To be honest, John isn't the quickest rabbit in the hole. "Well, to cut things short, she wondered where I got it."

He stared at me a moment, the color of his face morphing into the shade of a ripe tomato. I just hoped his famous temper wasn't going to show itself.

"Are you gonna bug me about that damn thing again, Matt? I told you I was sorry."

"No, it's not about—"

"It ain't my fault."

"I know. Just tell the lady what happened."

He shrugged, turned to Desiree, the redness starting to fade in favor of his usual pallor. "A couple of hours ago, my car stopped in the middle of the road and Matt here helped me push it into the garage. Only I accidently bumped into him and he fell into this thicket of roses. That's where he got the mud. The rain, of course, made it worse."

Desiree studied him for a moment. "I see."

John looked at me. "I'll pay for the damn dry cleaning."

I waved him away. "It's fine."

He started to take some money out of his pocket when a customer called him over and I was alone again with Desiree.

"Should I tell you what happens next, Matt?"

"Actually, let me tell you. I picked up the body after I, apparently, dropped it, then carried it into the forest and tossed it into the hole I'd dug. I covered it up and drove away, no one being the wiser—except, of course, for you. Is that about it?" I grinned at her.

"Yeah, pretty much. Except for me taking the pictures."

"Right, the pictures."

We sat for a minute sipping our drinks, neither of us saying anything, each just basking in the company of a fellow traveler making his way through this earthly plane. It was beautiful really. In a way, we really hit it off, even though this wasn't exactly a normal conversation. But you know how lightning kind of ruins the delicate beauty of a rain storm? Sometimes a person can say one thing and spoil the loveliness of a whole evening.

"I should go to the police."

That hit me the wrong way. We're sitting here having a pleasant conversation, and she goes and says something stupid like that.

"What are you bringing that up for?"

She gave me those puppy-dog eyes again. "Don't you believe that people should be punished for their crimes?"

I took a fifty out of my wallet and slapped it onto the table. I was getting out of this place and far away from her.

"Don't be mad, Matt. I'm not actually going to call them."

"I'm not mad," I said, looking for the waitress.

Desiree moved closer to me on the couch, her body touching mine. It felt nice. Still, I was upset.

She put her arm around my back and whispered. "Don't worry. Your secret's safe with me. I won't say a word. You don't have to kill me or anything."

I felt the air being sucked out of my body. I didn't whisper back. "You've talked to me for half an hour. You really think I'd kill you?"

"You see it in the movies. These assassins slaughter people just to keep their mouths shut."

"I promise I won't slaughter you." No waitress had appeared, so I stood up, about to go. "Well it's been lovely, but I should head on home, you know, with the storm and all. See ya."

I walked a few feet away from her.

"Don't you want to see the pictures? They're up in my room."

I stopped cold. Slowly turned around. "No, that's okay. I'm not interested."

I headed over to the bar to say goodbye to John. He gave me money for dry cleaning and I finally accepted. It wasn't worth ruining a friendship over.

I left the bar and went to the exit, when suddenly I felt soft, wet lips slide onto mine.

We kissed for a while, then entered the elevator. We took it to the fifth, our hands roaming over each other's body.

When we got to her door, Desiree stopped to look for her keys and it suddenly dawned on me that I might be making a colossal mistake. I remembered reading somewhere that men often take risks around beautiful women. But at that moment, I didn't care.

She kicked the door open with her boot, bit my ear and threw me onto the bed.

Later, we lay under the covers, Desiree holding me tight. I'd be lying if I said it didn't feel wonderful. She murmured something and then her eyes blinked open. She smiled, kissed me. "How are you doing, sweetie?"

"Good."

She rubbed my hand. "Listen, I kinda feel bad about something."

"Oh?"

"I lied a little to you before."

"I'd say you lied a lot."

"I hope this isn't going to change things between us. But you know how I said that I didn't want to make any sounds reaching for my glasses?"

"Uh huh."

She looked down. "I don't wear glasses. I have contacts."

I stared at her a moment. "That's what you're worried about?"

She nodded.

I laughed, then kissed her. "Forget about it. No biggie."

"Don't you have something to confess to me?"

I thought about it and realized that maybe confession is good for the soul. "Okay, you got me. I did it."

And you know what? I felt much more relaxed, not having to hide what I had done. And I'm guessing Desiree was calmer too. She's not saying much right now. But I think she's going to enjoy the trip up to the Vernasky Trail.

Maybe I'll take a few pictures of her.

Steve Shrott's mystery short stories have appeared in eighteen anthologies as well as numerous online and print magazines. He has written two humorous mystery novels (*Audition for Death* and *Dead Men Don't Get Married*) and a "how-to book" on comedy-writing. Some of his jokes are in the Smithsonian Institution.

JACOB'S LADDER
Cynthia Benjamin

David noticed his father's eyes first, unblinking, but full of surprise, asking a question that only he could answer. He leaned in to hear the words, his face so close to his father's mouth that his ears grazed his crayon-pink, glossy lips.

"How did I get here, son?"

David whispered the answer in a small voice that even his mother, standing next to him, couldn't hear. Then he placed the small wooden box, its lid covered with bits of shell and colored yarn, under his father's right hand, still warm to his touch.

How can his fingers still feel alive? David thought. *He's been dead for five days.*

David's mother pressed him close to her side as she said her last good-bye to his father. She didn't cry, not once. David overheard the neighbors call her "stoic," one of the many new words he had learned since his father's accident.

After paying their respects, another new word for David, they walked back to their seats in the front row of the funeral home. He looked back at his father in his casket, dressed in the suit he only wore for holiday meals and special occasions. David couldn't think of an occasion more special than your own funeral.

As they waited for the service to begin, the cast on his mother's arm scratched his wrist, but David didn't mind.

"I'm so proud of you today, Davey. I could never have gotten through this without you."

David buried his face in her side, trying to avoid his father's gaze, but it was no use. When he peered out, his father was staring directly at him.

"How did I get here, son?"

This time David didn't answer him.

* * * *

Seated several rows behind the Mitchells, Joyce Kilpatrick choked back sobs as she fingered the memorial program with Frank's picture on the cover. Such a handsome man, always smiling, always a kind word for everyone. A picture-perfect family, as they say. Sure, it was a cliché, but even clichés spoke the truth sometimes.

Joyce looked around the room, gratified by the size of the turn-out. Yes, advising Grace to reserve the larger room at the funeral home was the right choice. At a time like this the neighbors always pulled together. It didn't matter that the Mitchells had lived in their community for less than a year. They were a family in need, and for Joyce that was all that mattered. They weren't churchgoers, of course, like most of her friends. Well, each to his own was Joyce's motto.

Still, in their own way, Frank and Grace tried to be good neighbors. Soon as they moved in he volunteered to coach David's Little League team, and she helped out at his school. Of course all that ended when the problems with her last pregnancy started. Joyce nodded to some friends who had pitched in to help after Grace lost the baby, just three months before her due date. Tragic. She remembered how difficult it was for Frank to accept the loss. At the hospital he sobbed so that Grace comforted him instead of the other way around.

But David was another story. It was always hard to read that little guy. Her nephew, Matt, was in his fourth-grade class and said he was real quiet in school. Didn't spend much time with the other kids. Turns out he was artistic, like his mother. But instead of drawing or painting, David liked to make string figures. Some of the other kids made fun of him at first, thought it was babyish. But once he volunteered to teach them a few of his tricks they came around fast enough.

At the school arts festival a couple of months ago, Joyce and her sister were surprised to see what those kids could do with some cheap nylon string. Come to think of it, the only parent who wasn't impressed was Frank Mitchell. What did he say to Joyce?

"I'll never understand why David gets so excited about a damn piece of string."

* * * *

As the funeral service started, David thought about the last time he and his parents had dinner together. It was one of his lucky nights, when he escaped from the dinner table before his father could suggest playing catch. He still remembered what happened the last time they went to the park together. Even now the thought made his stomach ball up.

David managed to escape from the dinner table and make it safely to his bedroom. He locked the door, then picked up the nylon string his mother had bought him that afternoon at the hardware store near the mall. As he set to work, David said the names of the string figures his fingers weaved: *Jacob's ladder, witch's broom, cup and saucer, cat's cradle, star.* As his fingers flew through the air, he drifted to a safe, far-away place where his father couldn't find him.

But not tonight. When his father burst through the bedroom door, he filled all the space in David's small bedroom.

"You left the dinner table without saying something to me, son. Do you know what that is?"

David tried his best to remember. Please, don't let him scare away the right words, he thought. At the end of every meal he was supposed to say... What was it? Think. Think very hard. Pinwheel lights burst before his eyes, but still the words wouldn't come to him.

And then he remembered.

"May I be excused, Father?" Not "Dad." Never "Daddy." Always "Father."

Okay, good. He knew the words. That was the most important thing. Now all he had to do was repeat them to his father and it would end. But his tongue felt sandy, and his mouth was so dry he couldn't speak. No matter how hard David tried, the words remained tucked away inside his head, tumbling faster and faster until they split apart into bits of senseless letters and sounds, no good to him at all.

His father moved closer, his fingers tapping impatiently on David's desk, *rat-a-tat, rat-a-tat,* over and over. David could see his wooden school ruler only inches from his father's hand. He was thinking so hard about the sound of those fingers and what would happen after the sound stopped, that all the bits and pieces of words inside his head melted away. His father's tapping became louder, faster, first a drumbeat, then pistol shots. David wanted to stop the sound by blocking his ears with his hands, but that would only make his father angrier. Instead he looked down, his hands clutching the nylon string.

"One more time. What were you supposed to say before leaving the table? Tell me, David. Now."

He always expected his father's voice to become louder, but now it was so soft that David strained to hear him. When he looked up, he realized the moving fingers were still. The air in the room felt like damp cotton. It was getting harder to breathe; he was going to wet himself.

Oh, please God. Please. Just this once help me to say the right words. If you do I'll stop making fart sounds when Benny Leroy walks past our cafeteria table during lunch. I promise. Just help me make him stop. His father picked up the ruler in slow motion. Maybe there was still time. David paused and wet his lips. Sweat dripped down his back, scotch taping his tee-shirt to his skin. And then...he remembered.

"May I be excused, Father," he whispered.

"What did you say?"

"May I be excused, Father." David looked up at him, trying hard not to cry. Tears always made it worse.

His father slammed down his hand on the desk. David jumped.

"No. That isn't correct. 'May I *please* be excused, Father.' Get the difference, son? 'May I *please'....*"

David nodded, his fingers clutching the nylon string so tightly that it dug sled tracks into his skin. In another second his heart would explode.

"May I please be excused, Father." Was it over?

His father nodded as his breath slowed and his right hand relaxed. Then he dropped the ruler on David's desk.

Almost over, David thought. *Can't cry. Can't.*

Without warning his father's hands sliced through the air, tearing the string away from David and trying to pull it apart. But the thin nylon string was too strong for him. David smiled inside. *There are some things you can't hurt*, he thought, as his father balled up the string and tossed it into the wastepaper basket.

"What in the hell is wrong with you, David? How many times do I have to tell you? Damn waste of time and money. What can you do with a piece of string?"

Then he was gone. Only his smell remained. David picked up the string from the wastepaper basket and stretched it out to its full length. He rubbed it against his blue jeans to remove all traces of his father's hands. As his fingers started their endless dance, David repeated the names of the figures taking shape before his eyes: *Jacob's ladder, witch's broom, cup and saucer, cat's cradle, star.* Each one appeared and disappeared in a blur, faster and faster, almost wiping away the sound of his father's voice in the living room.

"I told you not to buy him any more of that crap. Not to encourage him. But no, you had to disobey me, didn't you? That's where he gets it from. The two of you, always plotting against me."

David's fingers stopped their dance and waited for his mother's answer. But she didn't say a word. Good. Better to say nothing and get it over with. Without warning his fingers sprang to life again, frantically repeating the same pattern: *Jacob's ladder, witch's broom, cup and saucer, cat's cradle, star. Jacob's ladder, witch's broom....* Saying their names drowned out his father's roar and his mother's single scream, high and sharp like an injured animal. Then silence. David looked down. The nylon string lay lifeless in his hand.

* * * *

Later that night, when the ambulance arrived, David was sitting at the bottom of the stairs, next to his father's body. All he remembered was his father's scream as he plunged down the staircase. When David found him, he was gasping for air, his eyes darting from side to side. David wasn't sure, but he thought his last words were a question: "How did I get here, son"? David didn't answer. Instead he called 9-1-1, just as his mother had taught him.

Later he watched while the two men from the ambulance tried to start his father's heart. If only they had asked, David could have told them not to waste their time. His father didn't have one. Finally they pulled a heavy zipper across his father's face until he disappeared into a black cocoon. David half-expected his father to reach up, unzip the black bag from the inside, and yell "Surprise," before jumping out like a comic book super-hero. But of course that could never happen. His father was truly dead.

* * * *

Grace Marshall saw the flashing lights from the ambulance as soon as she turned into the street. She had tried calling David from the emergency room, but when he didn't answer the phone she became frightened. This time she went to a different hospital, and it took forever to x-ray her arm. It was the right one and she wouldn't be able to work for at least three weeks.

She raced up the front walk, ignoring the neighbors who had gathered across the street. Her mind processed the EMTs with a stretcher in the front hall. There was a body bag. Was that the right term? But it was large, too large for a child, so it must be....

Please, let it be Frank.

"Is my son all right?"

"Yes ma'am, he's fine. I'm afraid it's your husband."

The EMTs looked uncomfortable, trying to distract her from the body on the stretcher. As if they could.

Grace waved away the rest of his words. Nothing mattered as long as David wasn't hurt. Then she saw him, sitting under the wide staircase, making those string figures he loved so much. That damn staircase was the reason they bought the house, even though they couldn't afford it. The way it swept down from the second floor, "like something from a movie," Frank had said when they saw the house the first time. And now that movie set staircase had killed him. He moved so fast, so heedlessly, especially when he was angry. She could imagine him running down the stairs, tripping, tumbling through the air, over and over. She touched her broken arm before pulling David to her side so tightly that he winced.

The EMT with the kind face had stayed behind while his co-worker wheeled Frank's body out of the house.

"Looks like he lost his balance and tripped on the top stair. Must have hit his head a couple of times against the iron balusters on the way down."

Grace nodded to show she understood. "I want to know exactly how my husband died."

The EMT paused and cleared his throat. "We'll have to wait for the medical examiner's report to be certain. But it looks like the fall broke his neck." He fumbled for the words he had probably said dozens of times to the truly bereft.

"I'm sorry for your loss, ma'am."

"Thank you."

"Is there anyone you can call, Mrs. Mitchell? A family member? Neighbor? We'll be glad to stay until someone gets here. You shouldn't be alone at a time like this." Grace realized he had misinterpreted her look of relief for grief.

"That's very kind of you. I'll call one of my neighbors. She lives just across the street. But first I want to put my son to bed."

As she and David walked up the stairs together, she noticed him fingering a piece of string in his sweatshirt pocket.

* * * *

When David pushed open his mother's bedroom door to say goodnight, she was already asleep, her injured arm making a strange lump under the scratchy wool blanket pulled up to her chin. He wanted to crawl in beside her under the covers, but Joyce said he shouldn't disturb her now. So he tiptoed to her bed and kissed her face, just under the black and blue mark on her left check. Then Joyce took him by the hand and led him back to his room.

"You're the man of the house from now on," she told him.

David wasn't exactly sure what that meant. Probably one of those dumb things that grownups say when don't know the right words for kids. Only he knew how important the right words were.

Inside his bedroom Joyce seemed uncomfortable, unsure where to sit or what to do. If only she would leave, he could practice the new string figures he had learned for next week's show-and-tell at school. David followed her eyes looking around his room, finally stopping at his desk where he kept his favorite book, a birthday gift from his mother. "Let's not tell your father about this," she had said when he unwrapped it. So David had been careful to hide the book at the back of his closet with the other special gifts his mother gave him.

Joyce picked up the book, which was still open to the page David had read and reread a few hours ago. He tried to breathe naturally.

"Now what's this one all about, David? More of those string figures you like so much?" She looked more closely at the diagram on the open page. "Well, doesn't that beat everything. It even shows you how to tie a knot with step-by-step pictures and directions." It took all David's will power not to grab the book from her hands. But he shouldn't have worried. Joyce put the book back on his desk, trying hard not to yawn.

"It's been a long night for everyone, David, especially you. Get ready for bed now. You and your mom have a lot to do tomorrow. I'll check back in ten minutes, so lights out."

Then Joyce bent down awkwardly, like a scrawny-necked chicken about to peck in the dirt, and put her cheek next to David's mouth. When he kissed it, some of her face powder rubbed off on his nose, like a dusting of brown sugar.

After she left his bedroom, David locked the door and picked up his book. Then he stretched out across his bed and studied the diagrams for the trucker's knot on pages 76 and 77. So simple to learn and so useful, just as the book said. He reread the description: "This trucker's knot is the perfect knot to use when tying rope or string between two objects, such as wooden posts."

Or between the spindles at the top of a staircase.

"This strong knot forms a very tight connection between the two objects, but it's also very easy to untie. Simply pull the trucker's knot in four places and it comes apart like magic."

Like magic, David thought, as he took out the piece of nylon string from his sweatshirt pocket and slipped it into the small wooden box, decorated with bits of shell and colored yarn. In the end his father was wrong.

You can do a lot with a piece of string.

✗

Cynthia Benjamin is a Manhattan-based feature film and television writer. She is also the author of twelve children's books. Her mystery stories have appeared in *Ellery Queen's Mystery Magazine* and two anthologies, *Murder New York Style: Fresh Slices* and *Murder New York Style: Family Matters*.

THINGS PAST

BK Stevens

He could have been saved, friends told her. You should have sued the hospital. But in those first days and weeks and months after Robbie died, Sharon was too lost, too numb to think about suing anyone. Robbie was gone—that was all she knew. She didn't care if the emergency room staff bungled things, barely cared who had stabbed him and left him bleeding in the street.

The police cared about that. They'd come to the house, drinking coffee and asking questions and then not clearing their cups away. She couldn't remember what they'd asked her—she could never focus on it. Hal had focused, and he'd gotten angry. He'd shouted at the police, several times. She had washed the cups and then gone upstairs to lie down. Eventually, the police had stopped coming. Nothing more had happened.

Now Hal was dead, too—just a heart attack this time, no police, no questions, no cups to wash. Now, there was nothing at all.

"Move here and live with us," her sister in Baltimore said. "We've got plenty of room, now both our girls are in college. You can look for a human resources position, and eventually you'll get a place of your own. You shouldn't rattle around in that big house all by yourself. You need a fresh start, Sharon. You need to make a break with the past."

The past is all I have, Sharon thought, but knew her sister was right. So she'd sell the house and give notice at work, and tomorrow she'd start going through rooms, putting things in stacks—keep, throw away, donate to Goodwill. She'd give the past up, too.

She got up early, resolved to get the hardest part over with first, and went to Robbie's room, wincing as she put her hand on the doorknob she hadn't turned in almost six years. Within seconds, Midnight was at her feet, squawking, butting his head against the door. No surprise. For over a decade, ever since Robbie picked him out at the shelter, Midnight had slept at the foot of Robbie's bed. Even when he started going to college, Robbie had lived at home to save money, and Midnight had kept to his accustomed spot. After Sharon closed Robbie's door for the last time, Midnight often paced outside it half the night, howling. Hal would curse, listing heavy objects he'd like to throw at Midnight, and Sharon would drowsily agree. But of course they didn't mean it. Neither of them would aim so much as a harsh word at Robbie's cat.

Now, Sharon took a deep breath. "Okay, kitty," she said. "We'll face this together."

Midnight raced in ahead of her. Sharon's first glance around the room gave her a jolt. The walls looked so stark. There was the Michael Phelps poster, and the map of France. But hadn't Robbie had personal photographs on his walls, too? Well, there were framed photographs on his bureau—Sharon's father and Robbie holding up the fish they'd caught that summer in Colorado, Robbie grinning as he showed off the two trophies he'd won at a regional swim meet, Hal and Sharon on their twentieth anniversary. Maybe those were the photographs she'd remembered.

She was surprised, too, to see three cardboard file boxes stacked next to Robbie's desk. What were those? She lifted the lid on the top box and saw the folded newspaper, saw the headline: "College Student Killed in Carjacking." These were Hal's boxes, the stuff he'd accumulated after Robbie was killed—clippings, copies of e-mails, notes. Hal sat poring over them night after night until she couldn't stand it anymore and told him to put them away. So this was where he'd put them. She'd have to go through them, see if there was anything she should save. But not yet. She'd deal with Robbie's closet first.

She'd known it would be hard. She hadn't been wrong. Even deciding whether to keep an old sweater meant being swept by memories and emotions she'd fought to keep at bay. But she pushed on. She finished with the clothes, crouched to look through miscellaneous stuff heaped on the floor, and came across Robbie's middle-school book bag. *This will be poignant*, she thought, and made herself open it, expecting to see mementoes from camp and Little League.

Instead, she saw things from college—framed photographs of Robbie with his pledge class, with four close friends clowning outside the fraternity house in an *Animal House* pose. Yes, these were the photographs that had been on his walls. Robbie's fraternity sweatshirt was here, too, along with a small cardboard box. Sharon opened it and drew her breath in sharply.

She had to sit on the bed, to open the box again and stare. Robbie's fraternity ring. He'd loved it—he'd worn it all the time. He'd been so proud of becoming part of Hal's old fraternity. For three years, the fraternity had been the center of Robbie's life. He'd never lived at the fraternity house, but he'd spent countless evenings and weekends hanging out there, and all his closest college friends were fraternity brothers.

Hal had been furious when they'd finally been allowed to see Robbie's body, and they'd realized the ring was gone. "Bastard," Hal had said. "He took Robbie's ring. How much was it worth? Sixty bucks? Could he even hock it? The watch my parents gave Robbie was worth three times as much, easy, but the bastard didn't take that. He took his ring."

And right before the funeral, when they'd had a last private moment with Robbie, Hal took off his own fraternity ring and put it on Robbie's finger. "This is for you, son," Hal said, and had to clear his throat. "Not only my son. My brother, too. No murderer can steal that from us."

But the murderer hadn't stolen the ring. Robbie had chosen to take it off, to hide it in an old book bag along with every other trace of his ties to his fraternity. Why?

She couldn't imagine a reason—couldn't think straight about anything, especially not with Midnight chasing back and forth, batting about some crumpled-up scrap he'd evidently found under the bed or nestled in a corner. "Calm down, kitty," Sharon said, snatching up the bit of card-stock. "Give me a minute."

She started to throw it away, then paused and smoothed it out. A memorial card from a funeral home, with a picture of a dark-haired girl named Veronica Kovach. Veronica Kovach—that sounded familiar. The picture seemed familiar, too. Hadn't she seen it in the newspaper, years ago? She looked at the dates on the card. So Veronica Kovach died at age seventeen, barely a month before Robbie died.

Sharon remembered now. The high-school junior found in a field behind a roadhouse outside town, dead of alcohol and opioid overdose. It had been in the news for days. No evidence of rape or assault, but the police had investigated and issued statements, trying to find out who gave her the alcohol, how she got the drugs.

And Robbie had apparently gone to her funeral, but never mentioned it. How had he known this girl? She'd been several years behind him in school. They could have met somewhere, of course. Still, it all seemed odd.

Sharon sat for another few minutes, looking at the pictures Robbie took down from his walls, at the ring he stopped wearing, at the memorial card.

She stood up. "That's enough closet-cleaning for today, kitty," she said. "I have to look some things up online." She left the room and didn't close the door behind her.

* * * *

On Monday morning, she called the college and made an appointment to see the Dean of Students. When she arrived, Kenneth Larson was waiting in the outer office. He was a tall, lean man in his early forties, his hair clipped short, barely brushing his forehead. "Good to see you, Mrs. Fahey," he said, shaking her hand. "Let me say again how sorry I was to hear about your husband."

She managed a smile. "Thank you. And thank you for your note. That was kind of you."

"Not at all." He gestured her into his private office. "Mr. Fahey was one of our alumni, after all—a loyal, generous one. Now. How may I help?"

She sat in the sleek wooden armchair facing his desk, half-embarrassed she'd come. "I'm moving to Baltimore," she said, "to be near my sister, and to—well, to make a break with the past, as she puts it."

He nodded slowly. "That sounds like a wise decision. But it must be hard."

"It is. Among other things, it means selling the house, and *that* means clearing things out, packing things up—you understand. This weekend, I went through Robbie's room, and I found things that confused me. I hope you can explain them, because I looked at his desk calendar, this silly cat calendar I gave him, and I saw he'd made an appointment to see you the day before he was killed. It's been a long time, and you may not remember, but—"

"I remember," he cut in. "It was the last time I saw Robbie. We had a good talk. He was a special young man."

"Thank you. I know he felt close to you—he often talked about how you really understood students and always supported them—and I know you were the assistant dean who worked with fraternities back then, and I wondered if Robbie talked to you about problems with his fraternity. Because I found things that made me think he'd dropped out, and I wondered if he'd talked to you about anything like that."

She'd sounded incoherent—exactly what she'd wanted to avoid. No wonder Dean Larson paused and scrunched his forehead before replying.

"As I recall," he said, his words coming slowly, "he didn't mention the fraternity explicitly. But we did talk about cutting back on extracurricular activities. He was taking the French Modernism seminar—that's challenging, even for excellent students like Robbie—and he was struggling to find enough time to do the reading. I asked if he was thinking of giving up swimming, and he said that's the last thing he'd give up. And he said he had to keep his part-time job, because he was saving for graduate school. So we discussed time management strategies. I gave him what advice I could, and he said I'd been helpful." He paused again, and his eyes grew moist. "Then he stood up, shook my hand, and thanked me. I remember that moment clearly—I'll never forget it."

Sharon's eyes got moist, too. She felt a rush of relief. "You think that's all it was—he needed more time for studying, so he decided to stick with swimming and his job but leave his fraternity?"

Dean Larson lifted his shoulders. "He didn't say that—maybe he didn't decide until after our talk. And he may have been growing away from the fraternity anyway. When he came back from that summer studying in Paris, he seemed—I don't know. More sophisticated. More focused on his studies, and his future. Did you sense that, too?"

"Oh, yes." Sharon glowed at this description of Robbie. "Definitely. Still, the fraternity was so important to him, and dropping out would be such a big decision. I'm surprised he didn't discuss it with us."

"Maybe he was putting that off." Dean Larson grimaced. "The fraternity was important to your husband, too, wasn't it? Maybe even more than to Robbie. Mr. Fahey never missed the fraternity get-together at our spring reunions. Robbie might've been nervous about how his father would react."

"That makes sense." Sharon thought it over, then shook her head. "But if he dropped out mainly because he needed more time to study, if he wasn't upset about something, why would he take his fraternity pictures down, and take off his ring, and bury everything in his closet?"

"You said it yourself." He didn't hesitate this time. "Making a break with the past means clearing things out, packing things up. I'm sure leaving the fraternity was painful for Robbie. Maybe he cleared things out and packed them up as a symbolic gesture, so he wouldn't be tempted to change his mind."

"Yes. That makes sense, too." Sharon looked down at her hands. This was such a comforting explanation. It would let her move on and not look back. But there was one more thing she didn't understand. She reached into her purse. "I found something else in Robbie's room—a memorial card, from Veronica Kovach's funeral. Do you remember her?"

Dean Larson squinted at the card. "I'm afraid not. Was she a friend of Robbie's from high school?"

"I don't think so. I looked her up online. They went to different schools. I can't figure out how they might have known each other, but he must've gone to her funeral. This card was crumpled up in his room. She was the girl found near the roadhouse, dead of an alcohol and opioid overdose, about a month before Robbie died."

"That's right," he said, nodding. "Now that you mention it, I do remember hearing something about it on the news. That roadhouse has always had an unsavory reputation."

"Yes, but the police said it looked as if her body had been moved, as if she'd died somewhere else, and somebody dumped it there, hoping the roadhouse would be blamed." Say it, Sharon told herself. She turned her face aside and stared at the floor. "And Robbie joked about how drunk people got at fraternity parties, and he said local high-school girls sometimes came by, looking for excitement, and I wondered—oh, it sounds impossible."

Again, he scrunched his forehead. "I don't understand. What did you wonder?"

Get it out, Sharon told herself, or you'll never forgive yourself. "I wondered if Veronica might've come to a party at Robbie's fraternity house, and had too much to drink, and got opioids from somebody. I'm sure nobody meant to hurt her—they're nice boys, I know that, and there were no signs of rape or assault. But if she overdosed, and they panicked, and they were worried about their futures and decided to protect themselves by covering it up, and if later Robbie's conscience bothered him and he said he was going to the police—could that possibly be why he was killed?"

Dean Larson sat back in his chair. "My God, Mrs. Fahey. What are you saying? That Robbie's fraternity brothers were responsible for this poor girl's death, and then killed Robbie, too? That they plotted it in advance—you *can't* mean that!"

"I know." She made herself look at him. "It sounds impossible. But the police always had doubts about whether it was really a random carjacking. I've been going through my husband's file boxes, the notes he took when we talked to the police. They said it looked like someone got into Robbie's car minutes after he left his job. Maybe someone he knew and trusted was waiting on his route home, and flagged him down and asked for a ride. If he asked Robbie to drive down that street by the old factory and started stabbing him, and Robbie pushed him off and made it out of the car and tried to run away—"

"Mrs. Fahey!"

Sharon held up a hand. "Let me finish. And this person chased Robbie, and then that truck showed up, and the driver saw what was happening and leaned on his horn and shouted he was calling 9-1-1, and the person caught up with Robbie and stabbed him again and took his wallet. Then he drove Robbie's car to where his own car was parked, and he took Robbie's GPS and the other things, and he threw it all away, dumped it in the river or something. The police could never trace any of it, not a single thing. So maybe the motive wasn't robbery. Maybe it was murder, to keep Robbie from telling the police about Veronica Kovach."

He stared at her. "Do you honestly think one of Robbie's fraternity brothers could have done that? To stab Robbie, and—no. I don't believe it."

"I don't want to, either." Sharon felt her face go hot with embarrassment. "They all came to his funeral, in their suits and ties, and they said such wonderful things about Robbie—it meant so much to Hal. But I can't make sense of it. Why did Robbie go to her funeral?"

Dean Larson sighed and handed the card back. "I don't know. He was so good-hearted—maybe he read newspaper articles, and felt sorry for her, and went to show his sympathy. Maybe she had an older brother Robbie met at a swimming event. I don't think she meant a great deal to him—he crumpled up the card, so he probably intended to throw it in the wastebasket. But he missed. He was a swimmer, after all, not a basketball player." He smiled sadly. "A crumpled card is no reason to torture yourself, to construct elaborate theories about why one of Robbie's fraternity brothers murdered him. Let it go. Let yourself move on."

"That's what I want to do." She stood up. "I may talk to some of Robbie's fraternity brothers first, to set my mind at ease. Several still live in town, don't they?"

"Possibly. I could check my files."

"Please don't bother. I have a couple in mind." She shook his hand. "Thank you, Dean Larson."

* * * *

She went to see Mike Dietrich first—another hometown boy, not one of Robbie's close friends, only a freshman when Robbie died, but Sharon had known his family for years. Mike was teaching middle-school social studies now. He pumped Sharon's hand and grinned.

"Great to see you again, Mrs. Fahey," he said. "Sorry about Mr. Fahey. My parents sent flowers—did you get them? Great, great. And Robbie—he was a great guy. Yeah, I noticed he wasn't hanging around the frat house much, the last month or so. But lots of upperclassmen didn't. Some had apartments off campus, and that's where they did their serious partying. See, people from the dean's office could drop by the frat house any time, to make sure we were checking ID's and all, and that could be a real pain. So if guys had another option, they took it. Veronica Kovach? Yeah, I remember that. Oh, man. That was something. The cops, the college—they were all over us, trying to find out if anyone gave her liquor or pills. But I never once saw her at the frat house, and that's a fact."

Justin Hughes also said he was glad to see her, though he seemed slightly reserved. He was a lawyer now, an impressive-looking young man in a tailored three-piece suit, his gray eyes serious and intense, his blond hair slicked back hard. Sharon hardly recognized the gangly boy who had been Robbie's best friend, who had cheered him on at so many swim meets. He met with her in his private office.

"Yes, Robbie once said something about possibly leaving the fraternity," Justin said. "It was just the two of us, working out at the gym. He was stressed about keeping his grades up—he had a hard schedule that semester, especially this one seminar with an insane reading list—and he said he might have to give something up. Junior-year grades are crucial for graduate school, you know. And he loved swimming and hoped to get to regionals, and he said he couldn't afford to leave his job. That's about all I remember."

"That's not surprising. It's been a long time." Sharon looked at the pictures on Justin's walls. There was the same one Robbie had taken down, the one of their fraternity pledge class. "You had an off-campus apartment that year, didn't you, with a couple of other boys from the fraternity? Robbie mentioned going to parties there."

Justin's smile was tight and brief. "Yes, we had some nice get-togethers, and Robbie was always a welcome guest. You know one of my favorite memories from that year? The time you and Mr. Fahey took us out to dinner after Robbie won the individual medley. That was a special evening."

"It was," Sharon said, but wouldn't be deterred. "I also wanted to ask about something else. Do you remember hearing about a young woman named Veronica Kovach?"

"Veronica Kovach." Justin knit his brows. "Sounds familiar. Wasn't she—no, that was someone else. I'm afraid I can't place—wait. Was she the one who died of an alcohol overdose at that redneck roadhouse?"

"Yes. At least, that's where her body was found."

Justin's brows relaxed. "That's right. I remember her name. Matter of fact, I remember it because Robbie mentioned it. He'd read a newspaper article about her. He said she reminded him of some girl he knew in high school, someone he had a huge crush on but never dated. He said reading about this Monica Kovach—"

"Veronica," Sharon said.

"Right, Veronica. Robbie said reading about her stirred up memories of this other girl, and he felt sorry for her—for Veronica Kovach, I mean. He got emotional about it. Did he mention her to you, too?"

"No," Sharon said. "He never did. Did he say he might go to her funeral?"

Justin shrugged. "I don't remember. It sounds like something he'd do—he was so good-hearted. Maybe he went to show his sympathy. Did you want to talk about anything else, Mrs. Fahey?"

"No." She stood up. "Thank you, Justin."

* * * *

She went to the police station next, and asked to see Detective Paul Baxter. He shook her hand. "I was sorry to hear about your husband. Please, have a seat. I've gotta say, I'm surprised to see you here."

Sharon nodded. "I know I wasn't helpful when you came to the house. I couldn't stand to listen to talk about Robbie's death. And my husband—he was probably rude to you, though he wasn't a rude person, not usually. But getting angry was the only way he could deal with it. And the only way I could deal with it was by shutting it out."

"I understand," he said. "You'd had a terrible loss."

"And now I've had another one." Sharon stared down at her hands. "I'm moving to Baltimore soon. Before I go, I want to try to understand what happened here. If you have time, could we go over things again? I'm ready to listen now. And I may have things to tell you."

* * * *

Late that night, Sharon sat in her living room, papers from Hal's file boxes spread out on the coffee table, a bottle of vodka and a glass on the end table at her side. Midnight lay in the chair that had been Hal's favorite, sleeping, his face pressed against the back cushion, his tail twitching sporadically. She picked up her phone and called Kenneth Larson's home number.

"Dean Larson?" she said. "Sharon Fahey. Sorry—I know it's late. But I was going through Hal's boxes, and I found Robbie's journal. I need your help with a translation problem."

"A translation—I'm sorry. I don't understand. Are you all right?"

"Oh, yes," she said. "Not quite sober, possibly. I didn't feel like eating dinner, so I've been drinking. For two hours, three. Maybe more. And I've been trying to read Robbie's journal. Did I tell you about Robbie's journal?"

"You mentioned it a moment ago, but I don't—"

"It's in French," she said. "When he spent that summer in Paris, this wonderful professor—Robbie adored her, said she was brilliant—told him to keep a journal in French and write in it every day. She told him to write about his experiences, his feelings, anything. She said it would build fluency. And I guess she was right, because he wrote a lot. Especially the last few days before he died—he wrote pages and pages then, and it looks pretty damn fluent to me. Not that I can judge, because it's been decades since I took French in college, and I'm rusty. Anyway, I ran across this phrase, *mauvaise conscience*. What do you suppose that means?"

"I don't know, Mrs. Fahey." He sounded deeply confused. "I took Spanish."

"Well, I took French," Sharon said, "and I think it means 'guilty conscience.' I'm rusty, but that's what I think. And there are several paragraphs about you—they say 'Ken Larson,' no need to translate there—and one talks about *mal conseille*. I think that means 'bad advice.' What do *you* think?"

"I don't know." His voice had hardened. "What's your point, Mrs. Fahey?"

"Robbie talks about Veronica Kovach, too," Sharon said. "He didn't translate her name into French—and I'm pretty sure that would've been easy, I'm pretty sure it'd be *Veronique*—it's a French name, isn't it? Originally? But he says 'Veronica.' I can't follow all of it, because I'm rusty, as I said, but I think he's talking about a party at an apartment, and about drinking a lot, and about Veronica passing out. Any of that ring a bell?"

"No," he said. "I think you've had too much, Mrs. Fahey. I think you should go to bed."

"Oh, I will. Soon. And in the morning I'll go to the police and give them Robbie's journal, and they'll find someone who can translate it, every word. Because you know what I think? I think Robbie and some of his friends tried to get Veronica drunk so she'd have sex with them. But they went too far, and she died, and they called you in a panic. And you gave them bad advice, and later Robbie had a guilty conscience."

"No." His voice was ice now. "That never happened."

"I think it did." Sharon pressed her hand against her forehead, closing her eyes, trying to keep things straight. "You were the understanding dean, after all, the one who always supported students, the one they trusted. Naturally they'd call you. And you were an assistant dean who wanted to be dean, and you knew you'd never be promoted if something like that happened on your watch, if a fraternity you were supervising caused a girl's death. You'd probably be fired, and no other college would hire you. The boys stood to lose a lot if the truth about Veronica's death came out. You could've lost even more."

"You're drunk," he said, and ended the call.

She sat silently, holding her phone, staring at it. Then she took a drink and leafed through papers from Hal's files. Half an hour later, she heard a knock at the kitchen door.

Dean Kenneth Larson stood outside. "Your lights are on," he said, "so

I figured you were up. May I come in?"

It's like vampires, she thought. *They can't come in unless you invite them.* But she stood aside to let him enter. Midnight came into the kitchen to see what was going on. He looked Dean Larson over, then checked his food dish.

She sat on the couch, and he stood facing her. "Give me Robbie's journal," he said, "and I'll ask someone in our French department to translate it."

Slowly, she shook her head. "You lied to me," she said. "You pretended not to recognize Veronica Kovach's name. But of course you did. When I spoke to Mike Dietrich, he recognized it immediately. He was only a freshman then, but it didn't take him even a second to place her name, because he said 'the cops and the college' were 'all over' the fraternity after she died. 'The college'—that would be you. You were the assistant dean in charge of fraternities. I'm sure the dean's staff had emergency meetings about Veronica Kovach. I'm sure you spent hours questioning all the fraternities. But you pretended you only had vague memories of hearing 'something on the news.'"

"There's no point in dwelling on this. If you'll give me the journal—"

"It's not as if you have a bad memory," she went on. "You even remembered the seminar Robbie was taking that semester. But you didn't remember something that must have consumed hours, days of your time? Please. Justin was slightly more convincing—but of course you'd prepared him. You called him and warned I might be coming, and you told him what to say. He reinforced everything you'd told me—not all the same details, but everything was consistent with what you'd said. A few times, he used your exact words."

He lifted his hands. "Honestly, Mrs. Fahey? You think I murdered Robbie, just to protect my career?"

"No," she said. "To protect your career, you told Robbie and the other boys to move Veronica's body. But that made it a crime, and you were part of it. You murdered Robbie to stay out of prison."

He looked down at the coffee table. "Is the journal mixed in with those papers?"

She took a long drink. "You can't have it. I hid it, to keep it safe. First thing tomorrow, I'm taking it to the police."

He hesitated, then took a gun out of his pocket, pointed it at her, and took a deep breath. "Robbie and the other boys were desperate when they called me. They begged me to help them, and I did. Maybe it was a mistake, but it's in the past. Right now, we're going to go get that journal."

She looked at the gun with an expression of mild interest. Then she shrugged. "Why should I? If I give it to you, you'll shoot me anyway."

"No. Without the journal, there's no proof, just the ramblings of a woman who drinks heavily and is half-crazed with grief and can't even read French. Give me the journal, I'll leave, and that will be the end. Think about it. Do you really want to give the police that journal? Do you want to dirty your son's memory?"

"I want the truth to come out," she said, "because that's what Robbie wanted. And Veronica's family—they lost a child, too. I'm sure they want to know the truth."

He cursed under his breath and drew his shoulders back. "I'm out of patience. One last time. This gun can't be traced to me. I confiscated it from a student, years ago, and never reported it. I'll tear your house apart, I'll make it look like a burglary, and I'll find that journal. You'll be dead for no reason. Now. Give me that journal."

In seconds, it seemed, the room filled with police—running down the stairs, bursting in through the front door, charging in from the family room, all pointing guns at Kenneth Larson and shouting at him to drop his gun, to kneel. He stared from one to another, and they kept shouting until he finally seemed to understand and obeyed them. Detective Baxter rushed over to take his gun and handcuff him.

"You should have waited," Sharon said. "I was fine. I wanted you to wait until he said he murdered Robbie."

"I didn't!" Dean Larson said, almost sobbing. "The journal can't possibly say I did."

"That's enough, Mr. Larson," Detective Baxter said. "Wait until we've read you your rights. Then we'll be glad to hear anything you have to say. Sergeant? Can you take care of that?"

Two uniformed officers led the dean away. Midnight strolled into the living room, looking indignant, and Sharon took him up in her arms. "Do you have enough evidence?" she asked Detective Baxter.

"Oh, yeah." He reached out to pet the cat's forehead. When Midnight hissed, he drew his hand back. "Enough for an arrest, enough to re-open the investigation into your son's death. Not necessarily enough for a murder conviction, but now we know where to look, we'll find what we need."

"Dean Larson *was* the first one to mention murder," Sharon reminded him. "Check the tapes. He said I thought he'd murdered Robbie, but I hadn't said that—I was careful not to. I only said he'd given the boys bad advice about moving Veronica Kovach's body. Until he showed up tonight, I wasn't sure he was the murderer. I thought it might've been Justin."

"Well, Larson was ready to murder you to cover up what he'd done.

That's a pretty good clue. And we'll identify all the fraternity brothers involved in Veronica Kovach's death—shouldn't be hard, at this point. Once they realize somebody's going to get charged with murder, the innocent ones should start talking fast."

"Not one of them is innocent," she said sadly. "Robbie wasn't, either. They all shared responsibility for Veronica Kovach's death, and for hiding the truth. At least Robbie wanted to do what he could to set things right."

"And I bet he tried to persuade the other boys to join him," Detective Baxter said. "I bet he told them all he was thinking of telling the cops. After he was killed, they all must've wondered if there was a connection. But not one came forward to tell us that."

She scratched Midnight behind the ears, feeling comforted by his low, contented rumblings. "I wish Robbie really *had* kept a journal. I'd like to hear it read out loud in court, and see those boys squirm as they listen to it."

"That would've been nice. Anyway, the journal was a great idea. I never would've thought of it, but it sure did the trick." He looked around the living room. "You gonna be okay alone here tonight, Mrs. Fahey? You've been through a lot today. I could get someone to stay with you."

"Thank you, but I'll be fine—a little shaky, but fine." She half-smiled. "Maybe I'll have some *real* vodka now."

She saw him out, closed the door, and stood leaning her back against it, looking around the house she'd shared with Hal and Robbie, the house she'd be leaving soon. She knew moving to Baltimore was the right thing to do. As her sister had said, she needed a fresh start. But she wouldn't make a break with the past. She'd bring the past with her. She could live with it now.

B.K. Stevens published over fifty short stories, most in *Alfred Hitchcock's Mystery Magazine*. Eleven of those stories are collected in *Her Infinite Variety: Tales of Women and Crime*, published by Wildside Press. She has won a Derringer and an Anthony, and has been nominated for Agatha, Anthony, and Macavity awards.

THIN BLOOD
Trey R. Barker

"…killed your first girl," I thought the old man said.

"What?" I froze, holding the café door open. My heart tripped, my breath blistered my throat, jackhammers worked my head.

And my nose bled. It was warm and sticky and tasted of tired copper. With my free hand, I put an already-bloody napkin to my face.

"Timmy," the old man said. "I asked if you knew that girl?"

The boy never looked away from me. "Yeah, Grandad."

"Well, she said hello."

"Hey." The kid waved absently, riveted by my bloody nose.

"Afternoon, mister," the old man said to me. "You all right? I know some first aid—" His eyes narrowed. "Have we met?"

"I don't think so," I said.

"You look familiar."

"See a lot of bloody faces do you?"

After a second, he grinned…sort of. "Uh…no."

"Somebody hit you, mister?" the boy asked.

"Thin blood." I swung the café door wider so they could trundle through and immediately their attention went elsewhere. I stood in the doorway, everyone looking at me even if no eyes were on me, until I saw Rita.

She motioned me to a table. "This is my section." Gently, she traded my bloody napkin for a towel that she pressed against my nose.

"Your section?" A small laugh jammed in my throat. "Don't you own this dive?"

"'Dive?' Come in here, bleeding all over, and give me sass? Hold that towel tight."

While I did, she brought me a soda, two cherries floating deep in the syrup.

I grinned. "Can't believe you remember that."

She shrugged. "So you get here okay? Didn't get lost?"

"Rita, I've been in town a time or two."

"Not recently."

A few patrons watched us and I felt as though every part of me was hanging out. Every mole and scar, every hair, every psychic scab.

"He gonna live, Rita?" the old man asked.

"No promises, Clete." She looked at me. "Reed, what'd he say to you? Outside?"

My grandfather's words—

—*killed your first girl*—

—stayed locked beneath my tongue although Rita knew them. Hell, most people in town knew them intimately. "He was talking to his grandson." I handed her the bloody towel. "Something about someone who walked by."

"A girl."

My breath hitched. "Yeah."

"And then your nose started bleeding."

"It was bleeding before that. Been bleeding a lot since I got his notebook."

She patted my shoulder, a touch as soft as a summer rain. "Right... because you've got nothing to be stressed about, nothing at all. Why are you rubbing your arm?"

"Ravages of old age. The baseball injury. Remember?"

"Hah! You mean when you got your cleats caught in second base on an ill-advised steal attempt during the state championship? Broke your left arm and cost us the game? That injury?"

"Ouch." I recoiled, but couldn't keep the laugh off my lips. "Yeah, that one."

"Hmm...feeling pain from a seventeen-year-old break that was in your *other* arm. So you're obviously still stupid."

"Apparently."

Her eyes danced bright and happy. "Damn, it's good to see you."

"You, too."

The old man, along with two or three of his pals, watched me. Not maliciously, not impolitely. Curiously.

"He thought he recognized me."

"You sure coming back here is such a good idea?"

Back in my hometown after nearly twenty years? Bleeding in Rita's cafe? Watching the old men try to figure out who I was? It was a terrible idea, but my head was murdering me and I had to stop it. This trip was the last idea I had. Nothing else—meds, every flavor of doctor I could find, primal scream therapy—had quieted the voices. Maybe going back to where those two men did such a terrible thing, where I believed the voices had started, would.

Rita kissed the top of my noisy head. "Welcome home, Reed."

Her voice trembled, a slight ripple in a calm lake, but she got in the car with them, her skin as pale as porcelain. She couldn't have been more than 16, still young and tender yet beginning to understand the world was not always peaches and cream. "It's all passed down, isn't it?" the driver said. He was older. The younger man was closer to her age so she took to him immediately. "You hungry?" "Yeah." "When was the last time you ate?" the older man asked. He watched her in the rearview mirror, shocked by the sky-shattering blue of her eyes. "Two days...when I left." They drove, the rhythm of the tires on the county highway lulling them while the whoosh of spring air through the car's open top warmed them. "Why'd you leave?" the younger man asked, dragging deeply from a joint. The older man had bought it, a few bucks spent on some joints that the man said would make the night go down smoother. He was probably right, but no amount of weed was going to stop the brain-splitting jangle of the younger man's nerves. He thought he might piss himself and was sure he'd blurt out the wrong thing at the wrong time and scare her away. "Piss on my parents," she said. "They don't understand." Raising her face, she set her jaw and the moonlight struck her. The driver nearly drove off the road, so mesmerized by the liquidity of light on her skin. "What don't they understand?" he asked. She grinned. "I'm an artist... not a teacher. Or a housewife." The driver turned off the county highway and onto a smaller road. Less traveled, less lit, more bathed in the glow of the moonlight. "But you're just a girl," the driver said with a chuckle. "Girls can't be everything." She sneered at the older man and turned her gaze to the younger man. "You can be anything you want," he said. She leaned into him. "That's damned right. It's 1976 and I don't have to do anything I don't want." She kissed his cheek. "Which means I can do anything I do want."

The trio drove and drove. The moon shone. And later, after some food, but before the moonlight began to stain everything black? She said her name was Polly.

It was about two a.m. when the town remembered. At least, that's when someone acted on that memory.

I was on Rita's couch. She had offered her bed and I'd wanted it, but not that night; maybe not even the first few nights. Deep sleep had been elusive since my middle teens and had disappeared completely since I got Daddy's notebook. My dreams, since my middle teens, were filled with the violence of what that bloody murder night might have been like. I had even inadvertently hit women before, flailing around in those dreams, and I didn't want to take that chance with Rita.

So I was on her couch, not sleeping, when I heard the deep rumble of a truck. It grew quickly and when it slowed, I heard someone grunt with effort. Then I heard the crash.

It startled me, but didn't particularly surprise me.

Glass shattered and the brick came to a stop at my feet, as though it sought me out. Rita yelped from her bedroom and dashed to my side, barely hidden in a thin tee-shirt.

"The hell happened?" Her eyes caught the brick, the broken window, and her head cocked when she heard the truck driving off in a blast of motor and a shouted "Freakin' killed Polly!"

"Damnit. That was Junior, wasn't it?"

"I'm sorry, Rita. I'll pay for it."

"How long's it been since you had a regular job?" She ground her teeth hard, but then put on a half-hearted wink, as though bricks through her windows were a nightly occurrence. "Don't sweat it, I'll take it out of Junior's hide."

Through dry lips, I said, "Maybe I should go to a hotel."

"And who, exactly, is going to give you a room?"

If they'd figured out who I was related to, then no one was going to rent me a room. We were probably lucky it had been a brick through the window rather than a Molotov cocktail.

"You're staying here." With a squeeze of my hand, she said, "Help me with this glass."

So I did, and for the rest of the night, for those few hours left before the sun cracked the horizon, she managed to calm my head and keep my nose from bleeding.

* * * *

Around 7 o'clock, the sheriff stopped by.

Rita snorted around a mouthful of orange juice.

Back in school, she'd been a beauty whose dreams of modeling had been her escape plan. We'd been friends, but never lovers, though that had been my secret fantasy. After the madness, I'd managed to scrape through to graduation and then I'd fled. She'd found a succession of crappy husbands but half-decent jobs and eventually she wove herself into our hometown in a way I would never be able to do.

Now we were approaching the hill of 40 years old and she was more beautiful than ever. The same face, the same velvet black hair, curves exactly where they needed to be. But a lifetime of experience and knowledge in those curves and her face. It was that experience and knowledge, the intellectual curiosity, that attracted me. If things hadn't become what they had, maybe she and I could have found something.

As the sheriff parked, she asked me, "How's your head?"

"Worse every day."

Rita smiled and pressed her knee against mine. "That's 'cause you're crazy."

"There is that." I emptied the highball glass of her homebrew and wondered what shape the shards would take if I smashed the glass against the side of my head. "The meds don't even work anymore."

Another comforting press of her knee and we watched the sheriff relieve the squad of his bulk. He moved slowly, an old man weighed down by a dead girl.

"Damn, can't he give you a few days to settle in?"

"He knows I'm here, Rita. I told him I was coming. He just wants to be done of it."

"I know. They all want to be done with it and damn whatever it means to you."

"Yeah, those selfish bastards." I laughed but she didn't. The pins and needles in my right arm had grown into a thousand cuts.

Sideways, she looked at me and whispered, "If your nose bleeds, bleed on those damned cheap boots of his."

"These are my best pair, Rita," the sheriff said. "Couple weeks' salary."

Rita filled my glass as fully as her face filled with angry red.

"A little bathtub bourbon? This early in the morning?" He stood just off the porch and the rising sun caught his face, painted it in harsh angles.

"Gonna arrest me for it?"

"You're not on my radar, Rita."

"I am." I drank deeply.

"Preferably not drunk." The man folded his hands over his belly. "You can't help me if you're drunk."

"Shouldn't help you at all," Rita said.

The sheriff sucked his teeth. "This how we're going to do it? This is an open murder case, Rita. Withholding information can be considered obstruction of justice."

"Open?" I said. "My grandfather was convicted."

"Your father wasn't and the body's still missing. Plus, your grandfather's conviction was four years after he killed her."

"And?" I challenged him, dared him to make the accusation I'd already fought with for weeks.

He didn't hesitate. "How many others were there, Reed?"

I leaned my head back in an attempt to keep the blood from pouring out. Christ, how much more could I lose before I had to be rushed to the hospital? Would the nurses give me a room or would they throw me out, too?

"He didn't confess, Reed," the sheriff said. "Because the Calley boys don't confess. We woud'a never known who killed Polly if not for that fire."

In the remnants of a fire at my Gramps' house, investigators had found Polly's charm bracelet. A few months later, Gramps was newly convicted and in prison.

"I know, Sheriff." I looked at him. "But I also know Gramps went to prison for life. Lost his life in prison."

Anger flashed across his face. "Lost his life? Like she lost hers?"

"Just as effectively," I said.

He stood as tall as his battered and overweight frame would allow. "Polly was murdered. He passed away. You get the difference?" His mouth twisted. "He tell you the stories? When you visited him in prison? He raped her, Reed, then strangled her. Son of a bitch stabbed her just to be sure. He was a goddamned monster."

He absolutely was, I wanted to say.

Instead, I stepped up to the man. "Shut your mouth."

"Yeah?"

Time stopped. Or maybe elongated. Or maybe wasn't affected at all. Maybe it just felt like it because I wanted to punch this tub of a man. Gramps' rage had passed to Daddy and then to me and had become a free-floating hostility that created the blackness in my head. Right now, the dull ache in my right arm be damned, I wanted to beat this little tin-starred lawman bloody.

"Reed?" Rita gently inserted herself between us. "Listen to me. I know you want— Damnit, you're bleeding again." She held her café apron against my nose and I smelled burgers and mashed potatoes. "I know you want to ride this idiot to the farm and back, and I'd love to see it. But what'll that get you? You'll go to jail and I promise that won't stop the voices."

The sheriff's right eyebrow rose. "Voices? A drunk who hears voices. Wonderful."

I sat and tried to forget how long I'd been tired. "The case was down 40 years ago. A man went to prison."

"And one went free," the sheriff said.

The silence was terrible.

Eventually Rita filled it. "And one beat himself up his entire life because of it."

"You ever see him again?" the Sheriff asked. "Daddy, sweet Daddy?"

"Hey," Rita said sharply.

"He got away with it." The sheriff pinned me with his gaze. "Gramps testified that your Daddy helped kill Polly, but he managed to slip away, didn't he? Never seen again." His voice dropped to a whisper. "Except you and me know he came back to town."

Rita's face was so sweet, aging angles and beautiful lines, but her fierce eyes ordered me to tell the sheriff to pound sand. "I don't...I don't remember seeing him again."

The sheriff spat. "Sure." After a minute or so, he took a deep breath. "Look, let's back up a little; start again. I just want to give Polly back to her parents. You said you could help."

Polly was in Daddy's notebook. He'd died a thousand miles and a lifetime from where he'd started without much to show for it. Some debt, some raggedy clothes, the last few days on a week-to-week lease at a Detroit flop, and a notebook. There were no dates in the notebook, no structure to the few pages of writing. It was clichéd and pathetic, though Mama always said he'd been a good man. At least until that night in August 1976.

The night of my birth.

Also the night of Polly's death.

When Gramps had shown Daddy how to kill a girl.

After that my father had been shattered glass. He'd been the shards I saw in every glass I picked up and imagined slicing deep into my delicate skin. His dreams, passed from his father to him, were just as violent as Gramps' and left him exhausted, but that shattered man had managed to get some of it on paper. Only some of *what* they'd done, but all of *where* they'd done it. When he'd died a few months ago, the flop house manager found my name, gave it to the cops investigating the man's death by natural causes, and they'd tracked me down.

"Reed?"

"I can help you, Sheriff, and I want to help Polly."

But more selfishly, I had to help myself. I hoped that, through discovering Polly, I could empty my head of the noise that had driven me spiritually deaf.

"Let's go, then."

Rita finished her orange juice. "I'm going to the café." She looked at me with those eyes I remembered from school, intense and almost bludgeoning. "You going to be okay?"

I kissed her cheek and twenty minutes later, the sheriff and I stopped for coffee. He went inside and I waited. I'd exchanged twenty or thirty emails with the man, each of us dancing around where Polly's remains were. I could have just told him but I wanted to be here. I wanted to be there when she was pulled from the grave.

I wanted to apologize to her.

Maybe that makes me a gentleman trying to pay off a family debt, and maybe that was partially true, but I also needed her to forgive me. I needed her to whisper that everything was fine, that coming late to the party was better than not coming at all, and that the broken glass in my head was going to dull over time.

The car door opened and I absently reached for my coffee. What I got in return was a hard slap.

"What the hell?" I tried to scoot across the car seat, but the squad's radios and computer stopped me. The hand snapped across my cheek again. A sharp sting danced on my skin. "Stop it."

"The crap you think you are?" someone asked. "Coming back here?"

My hand came up and I blocked a few slaps, but missed others.

"Why are you bringing this all up again? Why are you doing this to us?"

It was the old man from the café, face drawn and eyes blazing. "I knew I recognized you." Slaps became punches.

I grabbed his wrist, spindly and delicate, and held his hand away from me.

"Let go of me, you murdering son of a bitch." He yanked and pulled.

"It wasn't me. I didn't do anything." I held tight.

"Your daddy did. Your granddaddy sure as hell did. All you Calley boys are the same, murdering girls everywhere. Probably all over the state."

"I didn't do anything."

"How many bodies you got on your conscience, boy?"

"Damnit, I didn't kill anyone."

"How many?"

"*All* of them, you bastard." My voice slammed the old man backward. "Every girl they killed, don't you get that, you stupid son of a bitch?" My voice caused people across the street to stare. "*Every* dead girl is on my soul."

It stopped him cold. I'd never said that to anyone, even my ex-wife, who'd tried so hard for so long to understand my demons. My grandfather was convicted of killing Polly, but made a vague confession in prison to three more. My father's notebook intimated that wasn't even the beginning of it all.

How many nights had I spent thinking about Polly or the others Gramps confessed to or the hundreds more I imagined? Who were they? Did their parents still think of them? Did their friends even remember them? Theirs were the voices I heard, whispering and echoing. Locked in my skull, just out of reach, they were why I'd come home after so many years. If I helped get Polly back to her parents, those voices might just stop.

"Clete." The sheriff's voice boomed, an explosion in the still morning air. "Are you stupid? Get away from him."

The shock of my confessional leaked from Clete's face. He punched again. His arms pumped like tired pistons. "His daddy should'a gone to prison."

"Damnit, Clete, I know that. Reed knows it, too." The sheriff grabbed Clete from behind, pinned him between the car and open door. "Clete… Clete. Stop it."

Finally the old man quit fighting, his eyes burning, spittle dribbling over his lips. When he looked at me, he whooped. "I got you, you dirty SOB. I got a punch right on your nose."

Blood covered the lower half of my face.

"You proud of that, Clete?"

"Damn straight."

"Well, you can damn straight yourself to the jail this afternoon."

Clete gaped. "What for?"

"Assault and battery. Bring a hundred dollars, too."

"You're arresting me?"

"Clete, you can't beat on people because of their fathers. And if you don't present yourself at the jail? If you make me come find you? I'll charge you with resisting."

"This is bullsh—"

The sheriff held up a hand. "Another word and I'll take you to jail right now."

When he was gone, the sheriff glared at me as he climbed into the squad. "Why didn't you tell him? It would have avoided all that bullcrap."

"Tell him what?"

The car fired up and we headed out. "Damnit, Reed. These people need you."

"These people hate me."

He nodded. "They always will. Your Daddy and Granddaddy saw to that. But why not tell them you're helping? Let them know there's good fruit among those Calley boys."

I stared at the passing landscape. Desolate, filled with miles of west Texas nothing. This was the landscape of my boyhood and my nightmares. I hated that one of the last images Polly had was this land, lost of trees and built on scrub and mesquite and vast empty skies where a scream for help might carry, unheard, for miles.

"Listen," the sheriff said. "Polly is all I care about. I damn sure don't want your need for redemption fouling up my closing this case."

Everyone in town might well have wanted to find Polly, but they also wanted a pound of my father's flesh and since he was dead—and his death played big in the local paper—they wanted it from me. I might have been the innocent Calley but I was a Calley nevertheless.

My nose bled still. I pressed a towel against it and realized that once again, I had pain in my right arm.

* * * *

Two hours later we stopped about forty miles north of town, barely still in the county. We'd driven slowly the last miles and my head floated two different directions. There was no way I could know this was the right place. But at the same time, it was absolutely the right place. The scrub was different than my father's description, but it was exactly as I'd always pictured it.

My father had written of finding a girl, deciding on her with my grandfather, giving her a mix of sweet boy and bad boy just to get her in the car. Driving and driving, plying her with alcohol and weed, finding that perfect dark spot in the brush. He wrote of undressing her. He wrote of kissing her and telling her she was beautiful. He wrote of rape and strangulation.

He wrote of my grandfather saying, "You've killed your first girl," and "It's all passed down, isn't it?"

My nose bled and felt like gallons gushing from my head, splattering my shirt and pants. I tried to staunch it but it seemed endless, as though I was on the same blood thinners Mama had been after her heart attack. My right arm burned with exquisite pain.

"This is it."

"You're sure?"

I stared at the sheriff, then at the landscape, then at the man again, confused. "Uh…yeah. Absolutely."

* * * *

I've always had problems with my head. Things broken down deep amidst the ruins. What I felt about my father and grandfather; my anger at what they'd done and how that had affected me; what kind of life I might have had if they hadn't killed Polly; and the unanswerable question of how many they had actually killed. But this pilgrimage home, finding Polly, was going to fix my broken head.

I sat in the squad car and watched the sheriff direct two men with shovels and one in a backhoe toward the spots he and I had walked. He knew I didn't have a GPS location for Polly, but he also knew he was closer than he'd ever been, I could see it in his eyes and hear it in his wheezing breath.

As they gently dug, he came to me. "Never looked this far from town. Always looked closer to home…and in a straight line to his hunting shack." The man shook his head. "What's the connection to this place?"

I shrugged. "As far as I know…it was just a random place."

"Damnit."

"Sheriff, you can't detect and solve random."

"Sheriff?" one of the men called.

His face tightening, he went to the excavation. When he looked in, his shoulders slumped, his head dropped; the body language of relief. It was over. Finally and irrevocably, it was over. Gramps was dead in prison. Daddy was dead in a flop in Detroit. Polly was dead in the ground.

And finally everything, including me, was going to be okay.

She'd been in my head and heart for so long I needed to see the girl whose death had dictated so much of my life. So I put myself at the sheriff's side.

And realized his body language hadn't been relief.

It was frustration.

Because this dead girl wasn't Polly.

* * * *

"It's all passed down, isn't it?"

* * * *

I asked Rita to leave with me. To spend whatever life I might have left at my side, to help make something good of what was probably only going to get worse.

I remembered, not quite instantly, the dead girl. My head cracked open and everything spilled down my body into the puddle of my own urine in which I suddenly stood.

I held my tongue for two hours while the sheriff grilled me about anything in my father's notebook that might identify this new girl. So much smaller than Polly, so much more delicate than the pictures I'd seen of Polly.

"I don't know, Sheriff."

It was a lie. This girl wasn't in Daddy's notebook but she was deep in my head. Deep enough, hidden amongst the ruins, that I'd forgotten about her. Or blocked the memory of her. Or actively shoved her away.

* * * *

The town had lost its collective mind over this new girl. They demanded to know who she was and how she'd died, why my father had never been convicted, or even arrested, for her death.

"...*killed your first girl.*"

Mostly, they wanted to know how a girl had been murdered and they hadn't known it.

Her name was Bethany.

And the pain in my right arm wasn't because of an old baseball break in my left.

It was because of the cast on Bethany's right arm.

Daddy had snuck back into town for my 15th birthday. No one knew he was here, including Mama. We found Bethany walking along the county highway a few miles north of town. Her arm was covered in a hard cast which was itself covered in the graffiti of teenagers. Bethany said her mother had broken the arm during a horrible fight a few days before. The fight was why Bethany had left home.

Daddy had grabbed her by that arm and yanked it hard when she tried to get out of the car, and now I remembered her scream when the broken bones ground together. He yelled at me to drive faster so she couldn't jump out.

And then he said, "It's all passed down, isn't it?" He guided me into her and then guided my hands around her throat. "You've just killed your first girl."

Rita was stunned that I hadn't remembered killing a girl, that I'd dragged law enforcement to the very spot and shown them the very thing that made me a Calley boy through and through and that would get me a quick ride to the death chamber.

"But it was so long ago," she said. "Maybe that'll help. And your daddy made you...didn't he? Had to have. That's what he was taught so that's what he taught you. God, Reed, how could this happen?" She paced and smoked and swore at me. "Your nose doesn't bleed because of Polly. It bleeds because of this...this...what's her name?"

"Bethany."

She grabbed my face and I thought she might slap me. "Damnit, Reed, we could have had something this time. You were going to help the town get over Polly and we were going to move in together and serve everyone burgers and chili every day."

"I'm sorry."

She cried, and kissed me, and shoved a few thousand dollars in my hand. She told me to put myself in the wind and never stop letting it blow me along the roads.

"I could have loved you," she said. "Maybe that would have changed everything."

But Bethany was already dead by the time I met Rita. I was already my father's son...my grandfather's grandson...and my head was already broken.

I kissed Rita, hugged her, thanked her for the money, and slipped out of town during the night, exactly as my father had.

Because it was all passed down, wasn't it?

Trey R. Barker is the author of the Jace Salome series (newest addition is *When the Lonesome Dog Barks*), as well as the Barefield Trio. His short fiction has appeared just about everywhere and in every genre. He spent nearly two decades as an on-again/off-again journalist before moving into law enforcement in North-Central Illinois. He is currently a sergeant of patrol with a specialty in crisis negotiations and on-line child sexual exploitation.

TWO IN THE BUSH
John M. Floyd

Milo Stinson thought it would be quiet in the jungle.

He was wrong. The squawking and screeching and cackling seemed to come from everywhere at once. On impulse, he started hopping up and down and waving his arms, just to see what would happen. The forest—at least this part of it—went dead silent, the way it had done when he got here, ten minutes ago. When he stopped his jumping, the noise gradually picked up again, as if partygoers had taken time out to observe an interesting and puzzling new arrival and then returned to their conversations.

Stupid birds, Milo thought. He found himself wondering how anything could sneak up on anything in the wild.

Then again, this wasn't really the wild. It was a viewing platform beside a footpath at the Jefferson Park Zoo. He had even heard that some of the exotic birds in the two acres of tangled rainforest on the other side of the wire screen were former household pets, rescued and donated to the project. But it looked real enough. Winged creatures of all sizes and colors stared back at him from their perches in the green foliage, monkeys chattered in the canopy, crocodiles lay like muddy gray logs on the banks of the man-made stream. And though most of these woodland residents appeared to be minding their own business, Milo felt they were watching his every move.

Suddenly all went quiet again. Someone else was coming.

Milo kept his eyes straight ahead. He heard the newcomer's footsteps pause on the platform a few feet away. From the corner of his vision Milo saw a tall man in a black suit. He seemed to be studying the trees as well. After a moment the sound of the birds cranked up again. It was loud enough to make Milo's eyeballs throb in his head.

He said, still watching the forest, "Nice day for a walk in the bush."

"A little warm, for my taste," the second man answered.

How dumb, Milo thought. They sounded like secret agents in a sixties spy movie. But his instructions had been clear.

Having taken care of the formalities, Milo took a deep breath and said, "The name you want is 'Fitzsimmons.'"

The other man made no reply.

"Fitzsimmons," Milo repeated, loudly enough to be heard above the noise. "Oscar Fitzsimmons." He let a few seconds go by. "When do I get paid?"

"Tomorrow morning," the man said. Without another word, he turned and left.

Milo stayed where he was for a minute, his heart pounding. His hands were gripping the wire screen so tightly his knuckles were white. As soon as the birds reached peak volume again he left also, in a different direction.

The deed was done.

* * * *

As promised, the payment was waiting for him in his office the following morning, when he arrived at work. A brown vinyl briefcase sitting upright underneath his desk—he bumped it with his shins when he sat down. Inside the case he found four hundred grand in neat little bundles of hundreds. Milo didn't know how the case had gotten there and he didn't want to know. These people, and their methods, scared him silly.

But now it was over. With unsteady hands he closed and latched the briefcase, then picked it up and hurried down the back stairs to the parking lot, where he threw the case into his trunk and slammed the lid. He stood there awhile, leaning against the car and sweating and thinking hard. The temptation to leave now, to just climb in and drive forever, was almost overwhelming. In the end, though, he trudged back upstairs to his office. To disappear now, on the very day that the murder would probably take place, would be foolish. No one here at the newspaper knew yet what he had discovered—that was what had made his information so valuable. But if he suddenly vanished, right in the middle of things....

Besides, he wouldn't feel safe until the evening news. He needed to see the result of his little transaction. Oscar Fitzsimmons's death, which should happen sometime today, would mark the beginning of a grand new life for Milo Stinson, a life he felt he fully deserved, considering the risks he'd been taking lately.

With an effort he forced the subject from his mind and turned to a stack of paperwork.

It would be a long morning.

* * * *

His phone rang at one o'clock. He had just returned to the office from the deli across the street.

The voice on the line said only two words: "Meet me."

Milo felt cold fingers squeezing his heart. "What?" he whispered.

"The zoo. Same place." The voice paused. "Half an hour."

"I don't understand. Is something—" But the caller had already disconnected.

Milo's hand trembled as he replaced the receiver. The pastrami on rye that he'd wolfed down moments ago was making threatening noises in his stomach.

This wasn't in the plan, he thought. *This wasn't in the plan at all.*

* * * *

At precisely one-thirty Milo was standing on the platform again, listening to the noise of the forest beyond the screen and watching the monkeys play in the high branches. Or at least his eyes were on the monkeys. His mind was on other matters.

He stood there a full ten minutes before he sensed movement on the footpath behind him. Once again, the man's approach was greeted by the sudden dead silence of the jungle birds. Milo took a deep breath and turned to face him.

Although he hadn't taken a good look yesterday, Milo knew it was the same man. This time there were no games, no passwords. They stood and studied each other from a distance of six feet.

"What do you want?" Milo asked, when the clamor started up again. His mouth was dry, his heart fluttering in his chest, but he tried to keep his voice steady. This first long look at his "business partner" had done nothing at all for Milo's nerves. The man was tall and thin, his face cadaverous, his hands tucked into the pockets of an overcoat that was unnecessary in weather this warm. His eyes were as glassy and empty as one of the crocs on the other side of the screen. Milo's throat seemed to have closed up.

"Who else did you tell?" the tall man said.

Milo blinked. "The name, you mean? I told no one."

The man stood there and looked at him.

"You have to believe me," Milo said, his face heating up. "I'm the only one who knew, and I told only you." It sounded like a bad poem, and in his growing hysteria Milo almost laughed aloud.

The tall man said nothing. His cold, reptilian gaze never wavered.

"Why would you even ask such a thing?" Milo said. "What's happened?"

The man hesitated, then said, his lips barely moving, "The cops got to Fitzsimmons before we did. Now, instead of being dead, he's in custody. Probably being briefed right now about the many advantages of the Witness Protection Program." He paused. "My boss ain't a happy man."

Milo swallowed hard. His mind was racing. The birds, he noticed, were cawing and screaming again—he doubted anyone would hear a gunshot above all that racket. And no one was in sight anyway. This location had been picked by the tall man today, Milo realized, for the same reason it had been picked by Milo yesterday: it was remote and well hidden, especially at this hour, on a weekday. For an instant Milo considered running, then decided it would do no good.

Besides, why should he run? He was telling the truth. He'd kept his part of the deal. No one but Milo had known what Oscar Fitzsimmons had seen—except Oscar himself, of course. And Milo's information had been revealed to only one man. *This* man.

"I gave no one else the name," he said again. He knew he was pleading, whimpering almost, but he didn't care. "*No* one."

The tall man kept staring at him. "Then why'd they stop here yesterday, after you and me left?"

"What? Who stopped?"

"The Feds. We knew they were following you, even if you didn't. But I thought you'd lost them yesterday. There was no sign of them at first." He cocked his head, watching Milo's face. "Then two of them came here—right here where we're standing now—just after our little meeting. I saw them."

Milo was stunned. The FBI? He'd been followed by the *FBI*? For how long? Days? Weeks? Long enough, apparently, for them to have learned that he'd discovered an eyewitness to Congressman Ratliff's murder.

Oh my God...

"But why would they come *here*?"

"Good question." The tall man looked around. "It is, of course, a logical place to stop and chat awhile, if you happen to be strolling through the zoo. I considered that possibility. It's a spot where you can talk without being overheard. But I also considered that you might have known they were following you, and that you knew I knew. And that you might have left a little note here for them. A note with a certain witness's name on it—"

"I didn't," Milo blurted.

The man made no reply.

"I *didn't*, I swear it. I didn't even know anyone was watching us."

"I didn't either," the tall man said. "I wouldn't have come if I had. Like I said, they showed up afterward."

"And they stopped *here*?" Milo asked. "On this platform?"

The man nodded. "For at least three or four minutes. Then something happened."

"What do you mean, something happened?"

"I'm not sure. But something got their attention, made their heads snap up, like they just found something out. Then they left in a hurry."

"My God," Milo murmured. The implications of that....

But maybe they'd only stopped here by chance. Like the man said, it was the perfect place to talk in private. Besides, nothing could have come of it. "I didn't leave a note," Milo said again. "No note, no tape, nothing. I told *no one*."

A silence passed. "For your sake," the man said, "I hope you're right." He took another look around, then leaned closer. "Because my orders are clear, Milo Stinson. If there's any indication that Fitzsimmons's name was revealed by you, in any way, to *any*body..." Slowly, he withdrew his right hand from his overcoat pocket, just enough to show Milo the walnut butt of a pistol.

Milo's mind was in turmoil. Then, like beams of sunlight through the gloom, three thoughts locked in at the same time. One was that he would apparently be spared. There could be no firm indication that he'd told anyone else because he *hadn't* told anyone else. The second ray of hope was that if this man was going to kill him he'd have already done it, not waste time spelling everything out like the villain in a James Bond movie. His final comforting thought was that if the feebies had in fact been following him yesterday, maybe they were following him today too. Maybe they were somewhere close by, right now, with jaws set and guns drawn. His eyes darted to his surroundings, searching—

"They're not here," the tall man said. "This time I made sure."

For a moment neither of them spoke. Milo could feel his pulse hammering in his ears.

"I mean what I said, Stinson. In fact, I got a confession to make. The boss ain't just my boss, he's my cousin. Family. And I don't like people doublecrossing my family. In fact, I asked him to let me put a bullet in you today, one bullet's all it would take, and finish the job. I could even get his money back—I figure you probably got it with you, in the car." His soulless eyes drilled into Milo's. "But he said you deserve the benefit of the doubt. So again, I promise you: If I ever find out you're the reason that name got out, even by accident—even if you whispered it to yourself in a restaurant and got overheard—I'll kill you. One bullet in the heart, just one bullet, job finished, no questions asked. Understood?"

Milo couldn't reply. He just stared back dumbly at that evil, somehow fascinating face.

"Under*STOOD*?" Shouted, this time.

Milo gulped. "Understood."

A sharp squawk made both men look up at the brightly colored parrot sitting on a branch ten feet away.

"Understood," the parrot said.

There was a moment of stunned silence on the landing, then a look passed between the two men, a look of sudden realization. Milo remembered seeing the parrot sitting here yesterday—apparently the tall man remembered it too. And both of them now knew exactly what had happened, and what the Feds had heard, and who—or what—they'd heard it from.

An instant later the tall man's pistol was in his hand. A pair of explosions, one right after the other, shattered the quiet.

Finishing the job, it turned out, had taken two bullets instead of one.

In the moments after the gunman left and the smoke cleared, as Milo lay dying on the platform ten feet from the pile of bloody feathers, he was only vaguely aware of the frantic cackling and screeching in the jungle on the other side of the wire screen.

Stupid birds, he thought.

✗

John M. Floyd's work has appeared in more than 250 different publications, including *Alfred Hitchcock's Mystery Magazine*, *Ellery Queen's Mystery Magazine*, *The Strand Magazine*, *The Saturday Evening Post*, *Mississippi Noir*, and *The Best American Mystery Stories*. A former Air Force captain and IBM systems engineer, John is also a three-time Derringer Award winner and an Edgar nominee. His sixth book, *Dreamland*, was released in 2016.

THE BAD SLEEP
John Hegenberger

A death in Hollywood can mean a lot, especially if the deceased is rich and famous. But the death of a wannabe, a nobody, or a hopeful—even under extreme circumstances—can end up meaning almost nothing in this town.

"Okay. What's the gag?" The dark-haired guy almost knocks me over with the tang of his bourbon-laced sigh. "I get that you're a hot-shot L.A. PI, but I know damn well that your name's not Sam Spade."

I sigh back, perhaps too heavily. "It's Wade." I nudge my slightly-worn business card lying between the salt and pepper shakers on the aquamarine tablecloth closer to him. "Stan D. Wade."

People a lot smarter than James Garner have tried to read my kisser and gotten nowhere. Mine is an ordinary face, except for the streak of white hair that runs from my forehead to my crown. I stand five nine barefoot, and do my best to give the impression that I can take care of myself in a fight. It's an expected part of the profession. No one wants to hire a PI who might easily get sand kicked in his face by Charlie Atlas. The truth, unfortunately, is that I'm allergic to the L.A. smog and almost got an eye punched out early last year.

I don't enjoy pain, but it seems to insist on following me around, so I tolerate it as a sort of cost of doing business.

Today's business has me and Garner squeezed together at a slightly wobbly table in the back of Clifton's Pacific Seas Cafeteria. Outside, on Olive Street, it's a chilly January afternoon in the low 60s. Inside, it's a Polynesian dreamland that had once impressed Jack Kerouac. I'm having the fruit nut torte. My prospective client eats the bluefin tuna with pineapple. Around us, the walls and ceiling are decoratively painted and festooned with a south seas décor capable of ruining even a shark's appetite.

"You know, this is the very place that inspired Walt to design Disneyland." I toy with my fork, separating a brown-sugared walnut from a hunk of baked fruit cocktail.

Garner doesn't look around, but breathes more bourbon in my direction. "Well, it'll be closing for good soon. It used to be my favorite hangout, but the joint has lost tons of money throughout 1959." He holds my business card up to the light. "Where's...the Farraday Building?"

"Nowhere, anymore." There's no point in telling him it burned to the ground over a year ago and I haven't gotten around to printing new cards. "Did you want to hire me to investigate something for you, or not?"

"I'm, uh, thinking about it."

"Well, think faster." I make a show of consulting my dead brother's watch and then do a little name-dropping. "Marion Davies is going to be on *Hedda Hopper's Hollywood* tonight. I'm supposed to be her bodyguard at NBC."

Garner doesn't seem impressed. Just gives me a stare with his soft brown eyes. "I'll bet you read the trades." The actor currently starring in Warner's *Maverick* series lets a scowl crowd his glamorous features which, I consider, are not unlike my own. "I'll probably regret this in the morning," and he again sighs booze at me, "but I'm running out of time and am sort of desperate. How do I know if you're any good?"

Despite his hesitation, I warm to him and decide to play the earnest wiseguy card. "I'm like this city; hell, maybe even this restaurant. What you see is not what you get." That kind of statement usually sells them, or sends them packing.

Garner frowns. "Must be nice to work without a studio dictating your every move." He shrugs. "Okay, Mr. Wade, you're hired. I need a man to look into a murder that the studio says I committed. Jack Warner and his executive asshole, Steve Cromwell, are blackmailing me over it. Without cause, I may add."

"So you claim."

The actor grimaces. "A young screenwriter was found dead on the set at Corriganville. You know Corriganville?"

"Yeah, it's the outdoor standing set north of here." I fold my napkin and signal for the old guy who served our exotic meal.

"That's the place. Appeared as a backdrop in hundreds of B-westerns and TV shows over the last couple of decades. The writer, with the unlikely name of Chris Chandler, was discovered shot in the head by persons unknown. The studio quickly hushed it up, threatening to pin it on me as a way to manipulate me to work additional hours and days beyond my contract."

"I'm supposed to snoop around and find enough evidence to clear you or save you from the studio's abuse?"

The stooped-shouldered waiter comes over with our check and we look at each other for a second. Garner hands over a Diner's Club card and nudges my elbow. "You might even solve a murder while you're there."

He's having a little fun with me now, so I can't resist posing the key question. "Did you do it?"

"I figured you'd ask me that." He leans back, appearing quite at ease. "Of course I didn't do it." His dark eyes seem sincere. "Unfortunately, starting tomorrow, I can't go out on location for a few days. I have something more important to do instead."

His mention of murder doesn't bother me; I have contacts in the police force that are routinely capable of handling that sort of crime. His mention of blackmail isn't worrisome, either; the studios have been playing that dirty trick all over town for decades. No, what bothers me is his "something more important to do instead" comment.

"What's more important than showing up in front of the lights and cameras?"

He sips his bourbon and gives me a quick explanation, ending with: "Do you want the job, or not?"

I tell him how much I charge and wait to see if he'll change his mind.

The figure doesn't faze him. He writes me a check for the first week's retainer right there at the wiggly table. "That's how long I'll be unavailable, so you're on your own, Mr. Wade."

I like being on my own with other people's money. It helps me sleep peacefully at night.

* * * *

The dawn comes, and I take my sinuses and my T-bird for an airing past San Fernando, west through Simi Valley, while listening to "Shimmy Shimmy Ko Ko Bop" on the car radio. A catchy tune, indeed, but I turn down the volume when the car phone buzzes.

I speak into the jury-rigged device that my pal, Norman, has built into the Ford's dashboard. "To be honest, I don't know why I took the case," I lie to Suzi.

Her tinny voice comes back to me from the contraption's speaker. "We don't need the money, Standy. The agency is back in the black and doing well ever since that Jerry Lewis investigation."

"I know. I just don't like the way the major studios still think they can push talent around, that's all. Edd Byrnes and Clint Walker both bumped heads with Jack Warner last year. Now Garner says he's getting threatened by the same outfit. Plus…there's supposed to be a dead body involved."

"Standy, promise you'll be careful. I know you haven't been sleeping well lately, and I suspect that you're on one of your crusades again."

What a sweetheart! I bid her bye and turn the wheel, steering through Suzanna Pass. Marty Robbins is now crooning about El Paso. I wonder if I'll catch sight of one of those new Nike missile installations out here. They're designed to pop up from an underground bunker and roar into the sky, day or night, to take out enemy airplanes. Ever since the middle of the Cold War, whole families come out on the weekends and picnic in the area with peanut-butter-and-jelly sandwiches, hot dogs and ants, hoping to see the silos open and the rockets elevate. What a nightmarish image!

I've been having a lot of sheet-clenching nightmares of my own the last few months. None of them had giant ants or rocket explosions, fortunately. Not long ago, I'd intentionally killed someone for the first time—a woman who was about to kill me—and ever since, I'd begun to suffer through troubled sleep. I guess it could be worse; I could be as dead as the guy in this case Garner wanted investigated. A little bad sleep is better than the big sleep any day.

Coming out of the Santa Suzanna Mountains, north of Los Angeles, I run into three miles of heavy construction along Highway 118. I get to spend a little time staring at stands of cottonwood trees along the roadside. A sodden, cloud-congested sky lends an uneasy dimness to the day. The wind rips wildly against the higher branches like a cataract pouring into a chasm.

Suzi may have been right about my being on a sort of crusade. Guilt has a way of making a fella do fascinating and foolish things.

* * * *

Around forty-five minutes later, I arrive at the entrance to the western backlot and see that the place has been converted into a weekend tourist trap. Here families can "visit an authentic western town" and even witness an "authentic shootout." What Disney and Marineland have done for fantasy and ocean-view theme parks, Corriganville is trying to do for the cowboy experience, complete with "authentic horse shit."

The guard stationed at the entrance to the grounds wears his hat far back on his head and twirls a rope to get visitors into the western spirit. I show him a note that Garner had scribbled, and the friendly shitkicker lets me pass, casually spitting tobacco juice on my left front hubcap. I drive slowly, eventually finding the movie set portion of the ranch, and park beside a row of dark-blue electrical trucks that house the generators to power huge banks of lights and a couple of enormous wind machines.

The true reason I've taken the case is that it gives me a chance to spend time with celebrities; especially those from my youth. I've always have been a sucker for movie stars, ever since the days I'd sat in the balcony of the Jewel Theater and watched westerns and serial chapters flash across the big screen. Hell, I'd once worked as a stuntman at Republic

Studios in order to appear in the background of low-budget oaters.

In these intense days of civil defense bomb shelters, Supreme Court racial rulings, and alarming nightly news programs, everybody needs a distracting hobby. Other people collect autographs; I collect behind-the-scenes experiences and backstage relationships with film personalities. This Corriganville investigation gives me an excuse to again feel like I'm a part of those fun and foolish movies. So sue me.

And here, coming toward me, is a new old Hollywood star: Ray "Crash" Corrigan. He's wearing a long-sleeve tan and red cowboy shirt embroidered with white roses. His wide-brimmed hat has a scarlet cord around the crown. "You the dude that Garner sent?'

Growing up, I hadn't taken much notice of Ray Corrigan, since he wasn't as big a star as Roy Rogers or Hopalong Cassidy, but his face is familiar, since he played beside John Wayne in a handful of "Three Mesqueteers" features.

He'd put on about fifty more pounds since he'd played in his western movies, but the face was still familiar and he sat a horse with ease. When he grinned and glad-handed you, you just had to smile back. At least I did, anyway.

I'd heard that he'd invested well in the early 1950s by creating this little ranch and western village for use as a busy backdrop in the production of horse operas. Then, when television had blossomed, the place got even busier, until finally the aging cowpoke actor got the idea of opening it up so the public could walk the dusty streets of what felt like an old western town.

I show him the note from my actor/client and watch the big man carefully while he reads it. When he asks why Garner's not with me, I mention client confidentiality and smile convincingly, I hope.

Never one to turn down a role in a movie, Ray had kept his name in the credit crawl of several movies by continuing to play a second-string cowboy and even a costumed gorilla. Since then, he has used his notoriety to advantage with his self-named theme park.

Corrigan hands the note back to me, appearing perturbed and even a might guilty. He jerks a thumb down the main street to a small building behind the livery stable. "The body was found inside there…supposedly."

I step over the threshold of the equipment shed he's indicated and immediately feel the increased temperature within the enclosed space. Ray pauses in the doorway to slap dust off his boots. "Despite this being early January, the temperature in here is as hot as a July jalapeño."

I decide to verbally play along. "And as dry as an August arroyo."

He lets that one settle.

Standing inside this hot shack, sweat begins to form above my eyes; slowly they adjust to the darkness. I see a jumble of workman tools, camera and sound gear, and a few broken props piled in the far corners of the single-room building. Tangles of cables, a stand of Klieg lights, a broken boom mic, a seven-inch reel tape recorder and an electrical switch box that likely was left over from *The Bride of Frankenstein*, and yes there's an irregular dark spot on the bare floor that has to be dried blood. Dread clings to me like cobwebs.

I swallow carefully and poke around a bit more. The metal power conduit box lays flat on its back, trailing wires beside a stack of reflector panels and an old-time camera still locked into place on its tripod. Is that a tarnished timpani drum?

Still puzzled, I turn back to look at Ray's dark, hulking outline framed by the sunlight in the open door. "Any idea why the crime was committed here?"

"It's a secluded and controlled space." He scrapes the soul of his boot against the door frame. "The studio likes to have a controlling interest."

"What do you mean?"

He shrugs. "They want to stick it to the actors and writers. I'd side with Garner about fighting those corporate vultures, but I can't afford to lose this-here ranch or the filming business it brings in. Best if I stay out of it."

The fond recollection of a childhood hero pops like a soap bubble. The image of Corrigan as a brave, courageous, and bold cowboy takes a mental beating. Or maybe I'm just tired from lack of sleep. Either way, I figure Corrigan's not the killer, since his sympathy lies with the little man and his fears originate from the corporations that are getting larger every day.

Maybe it's the outfit I'm wearing that inspires me to give Ray a little advice: "My old pappy used to say, 'The bigger they are, the smaller they're hard.' If we don't stand up against the big guys, who will?"

He grunts and gives me a hard stare. "Very clever, Mr. Maverick."

We stroll outside into the sunlight. Since the park was open to the public during the weekends, I know that Corrigan has at least one source of income that's not directly under the studios' control. I wonder just how profitable the place is. "Mind if I wander around a bit?"

He grins with ease and saunters off without another word.

I'm left feeling like my eleven-year-old self, back at the summer dude ranch where I'd watered, fed, and curried my first horse. I'd been one with nature and the old west. That first ride out of the white-slatted corral and along the dirt trail up the side of a shaded hill had made a new kid of me back then. Like being baptized.

You see a lot of western towns on television these days. All of them have rough-hewn hitching posts, leaking watering troughs, dusty board-walks, and saloons with tinny pianos, general stores with cracker barrels, pickle jars, and black pot-bellied stoves. Gazing around this mock cowboy setting, I recall that director John Ford once used Corriganville as the main set for his film, *Fort Apache*.

A buckboard rattles in my direction and something—maybe a hornet—causes the horse to rear up beside me, pushing the back of my calves over the upper edge of a watering trough. Instantly I'm plunged, soaked and startled, splashing and gripping rough wet wood, cursing like a three-legged bobcat. *Baptized, again.*

The driver, an old gal in calico, rides on oblivious, and leaves me to sputter and fend for myself. At the far side of the near-empty clapboard Cowtown, under the shade of a grove of oaks, I drip my way to a small circle of trailers and silver motorhomes. One of them has Garner's name taped beside the door. The key that he'd given me fits the lock and I clamber inside.

Still cursing quietly to myself, I change into one of his dry western outfits and look in the mirror. There's a handsome man in there, dressed as a gambling dude with string tie, ruffled shirt, trim vest, and black hat cocked at the back of my head. I give the mirror a winsome smile. "Howdy, ma'am. My handle is Wade. Bret Wade."

The mirror is delighted to make my acquaintance.

What the hell; why not go whole hog? I find a gun belt and begin to buckle it on my hip when I realize my trousers have been designed for a ballet dancer. There's no zipper in the crotch. Now, of course, that very thought causes me to want to empty my bladder.

I have the tight pants down around my ankles and am seated on the trailer's throne when I hear the front door pop open and muffled footsteps shuffle across the floor. I shimmy-shimmy back into my pants and come out of the cramped bathroom to see the tail end of some dude whisking back out the door.

A sheet of paper has been dropped onto the sofa and I pick it up. While unfolding the note, I catch a glimpse out the trailer window of the top of the redheaded dude who'd delivered it.

The handwritten message reads: *Final warning. Get to work or go to jail for murder.*

I crumple the paper in my fist as I dash out the trailer door in pursuit of the messenger.

As soon as I catch up, I reach out and swing the guy around to face me. His eyes are tight and blue, his expression worried. But there is an ingratiating charm to his face, boyish under a pile of sandy hair. He appears harmless, but I know that handsome looks can conceal a cruel temperament, especially in Hollywood.

I lean in on him to prove that even if I'm dressed silly, I mean business. "What's the idea?"

His eyes search for a way out of the confrontation. Then he eases back and gives me a half smile. "What do you mean?"

"Who are you?" I hold up the scribbled note so he'll have to stare at it. "What's the idea of this?" I thrust my right hand, clutching the paper, at his chest.

Somewhere behind us, a mule starts braying, and the redhead puts his hands up as if to push me away. His smile grows wider. Suspicion is no longer in his crinkled eyes. Just a nice guy out for a stroll. "Bobby Redford's the name." He sticks out his hand glad-to-meet-me. "What's this all about, officer?"

Yes, sir. A swell guy. And he thinks I'm a cop, which is probably due to my gruff manner. I should use it more often. So I don't shake hands with him. Instead, I give him a stern look. "You an actor?"

He puts his hands down and leans back against a weathered hitching post. "I try to be. I'm in the episode of *Maverick* we're filming here. Guy gave me that message to put in Mr. Garner's trailer. Said it was important."

"What guy?"

He looks away, thinking. "The guy who works as an enforcer at Warners. He thinks he's a cop, too. So naturally, I...."

I know who he's talking about and quickly give him a description of Mr. Steve Cromwell, chief fixer for Jack's studio.

"Yeah, him. Why are you so steamed, officer? I've been hearing talk around about Chris Chandler getting shot."

"You know about that?"

The pretty boy puts his hands in his back pockets. "Yeah, I ran into him a couple of times in the equipment shed. I practice and play back my lines sometimes on an old tape recorder in there. He gave me a couple of pointers once from a screenwriter's perspective. Nice little guy. Sorry to hear about the shooting and all."

"Do you know who did it?"

Redford rubs the back of his neck. "Why would I know a thing like that?"

"Okay, then. Did Chandler ever seem nervous, or act funny?"

"All writers seem funny to me. Chris talked a lot about the pending

Writer's Guild strike, if that matters. Guy wasn't sure if he'd walk the picket line or not."

If Redford said "guy" one more time, I'd belt him. "Did Chandler ever mention feeling threatened by anyone?"

"I really don't recall. I usually didn't pay much attention to his nutty ramblings. Sorry."

I decide that Redford has a good shot at making it to the top of his profession, if he maintains that boyish grin. I doubt that he's a killer.

His eyes dart over my left shoulder. "Speak of the devil. Over there's the guy who had me deliver that note."

I turn to see Cromwell stepping slowly toward us. His wingtips are polished even out here in the middle of a fake one-horse town. His hands are raised, open-palmed, as if someone is holding a gun on him; one hand holds a burning cigarette. He seems calm and confident, like he thinks he owns the place.

Redford uses the opportunity to back away and I let him. Cromwell comes closer; collar is open, striped tie loose. His intense expression disappears momentarily behind a cloud of cigarette smoke. "You Wade?"

I nod.

"You're dressed awfully funny for a private investigator, fella." His voice is husky with a little catch in it, which is probably due to too many coffin nails and all that East Coast money. "Yeah peeper, I know who you are and why you're here. Keep sticking your nose in and we'll sue it off."

"I've heard that one before and it doesn't faze me." I hold up the sheet of paper delivered by Redford. "Did you write this?"

He shakes his head, but I'm certain that he's lying. "Let me give you a little tip, Wade. Finding talent in Hollywood is not a problem. Controlling it is the secret to success in this town."

"And you tried to control Chandler, but he wouldn't cooperate, right? Now you're trying to use his death to keep Garner in line."

The bureaucrat folds the paper, moving it to the inside pocket of his suit coat. "The studio doesn't give a rat's ass about some dime-a-dozen writer. Even a good one, like Browne, there." He points to a gray-haired guy in a baggy suit, standing under the awning of the Assay Office. "Like I said, keep out of this, fella, or you'll wind up in court." He walks away.

I let him go, because I'm more interested in talking with the writer he's pointed out. I'd met Howard Browne a couple years earlier when he'd hired me to give him background and local color for a screenplay he was developing. In the Forties he penned a series of "Halo" novels about a Chicago PI named Paul Pine. Good stories, and now I hear he's some sort of story editor at Warners. Garner was right; I read the trades.

As I approach, Browne glances my way over the tops of his bifocals. His face is round and his build is stocky, broad-shouldered. He has a script open in his hands. If anyone knows what happened to Chandler, it's bound to be a fellow writer like Browne.

After I hail him and shake his moist hand, he wants to know why I'm dressed up like Maverick. I dodge the question and ask him about the young writer, Chandler.

"Yes, he seems a dedicated, hard-working cuss. A little moody, effeminate and a bit stand-offish, but probably Hollywood's next best hope, you know? I haven't seen him a couple of days."

"You haven't heard?"

"Heard what?"

"The word on the street is that your pansy writer's been murdered. Ask Corrigan. I think he found the body."

"What! That's terrible. I thought maybe he'd gone off to picket with the WGA, since he is, or was, a staunch union member. Damn! Now I'll have to get Wells Root to re-write the scenes we still need to shoot."

"Would the Writer's Guild be able to give me any background on him? Where he lives? Other people who knew him?"

"If you want to know stuff like that, you should ask Dobie. They often spent time together, I hear."

"Dobie? You mean Harry Carey, Junior?"

Browne gestures with his rolled script. "That's him over by the sheriff's office and town jail."

So it is.

* * * *

"Howdy."

Dobie Carey wears a western-cut sport coat with pads at the elbows and a maroon shirt with flowered tie. He's the son of actor Harry Carey. Both men have appeared in dozens of westerns, although seldom together. He's called Dobie because of his red hair, now thinning and faded to russet-blond. His nickname is short for adobe, like the color of New Mexico clay at sunset, or at least that's what I'd read in the trades.

We stand on the boardwalk watching three cowpokes stroll past, strumming guitars and torturing a squeeze box. The clouds behind them are silver. Spun glass rain is blowing in the west.

"I should have seen it coming." He wipes perspiration from his high forehead with the tip of his tie. "I'm here filming location scenes for a Jim Davis western, *Noose for a Gunman*. Chris and I ate lunch together over by the lake. But are you sure that she's dead?"

I stare at the Wanted posters on the wall outside the sheriff's office. One of the sketches looks alarmingly like Walt Disney. Distant lightning strikes and I taste the smell of fresh-clipped grass, or maybe it's a reefer. "She?"

"Oh, that's a mistake." He breathes a sigh at me, just like Garner had. "Well, anyway ...."

"She? Chandler's a woman?"

He shrugs. "Dressing like a man helped her get work from the studio execs. Adopted a masculine name, like Leigh Brackett. Christine hated doing it, but called a 'necessary evil' in that deep Tallulah voice of hers."

I must be slipping. A good private investigator would have figured that out by now. I decide to blame the gaff on my lack of sleep. I tip my hat to Dobie like he's the best friend I have on earth.

He grins back. "Hope I helped. Gotta run. Davis needs me for a big gun-down scene."

* * * *

By day's end, I've confirmed that Corrigan was the person who had found the body and that he'd immediately informed Cromwell, who had taken it from there. The question is: taken it where? I go back to the equipment shed for a second look around. Among the saws, pipes, wires, and camera parts, a small Movieola sits next to a brown bottle of Vitafilm, a liquid used to keep film fresh and limber as it passes through the editing device's gate. Nasty smelling stuff.

Dobie wasn't the only redhead in this affair. Redford had mentioned using the tape recorder. Maybe he wasn't the only one who'd recorded things on it. I switch on the machine and run the tape forward and back a few times over Redford's voice, until the end. The tape runs out and I turn it over and re-thread it to play the other side. I hear a strong female voice say: "This is Christine Chandler speaking and I'm about to take my own life in protest. The studio slavery system must end. Let this act shine a light on the shadowy dealings of the crooks at the top of the system." I get that chill at the base of my skull, because I know what's coming. Still, I flinch at the loud report of gunfire.

"I'm sorry you had to hear that, Mr. Wade." Cromwell's voice behind me is harsh and sharp.

I face around and see he's holding a hatchet in his right hand. I try to mask my surprise with confrontation. "You knew all along about the suicide. Where's the body? And the gun?"

"All taken care of, fella." He moves in toward me.

"Sure. Except for this." I point to the recorder which has shut down now that the tape had ended. "You didn't know that she'd recorded a suicide note before shooting herself."

"She?"

"Fooled you too, eh? Even though you must have seen the body. Where'd you stash it?"

I take advantage of his confusion to throw a carpenter's hammer at his face.

He ducks and comes at me with the short ax raised.

I fight back with a screwdriver. It's the only sharp thing I can lay hands on.

The blade chops down, pinning the right sleeve of my western costume to the edge of a wooden table. Equipment parts and tools sail high, tumbling and clanging near my head. The bottle of Vitafilm strikes the planked floor and shatters into a rank, glittering puddle. The harsh stink envelopes us.

I cough, clutch the cool neck of the broken bottle, and now have a sharp weapon in each hand.

But the blade of the hatchet is wrenched free from the table just as I get to my feet. I bite my lower lip. The bitter blood and tawny odor makes me woozy, but I dodge left, past a broken tripod to thrust my hip into the side of the table, sending it and the tape recorder skidding into Cromwell. The hatchet is heavy enough to take him off balance. I stumble through the fumes, swishing the screwdriver at his head. I catch a knee in my chest for my trouble and slam back on my ass. The cost of doing business.

He laughs. "Everything's been taken care of...except you and that tape."

The door opens behind us and I see a gorilla lumber in and grasp Cromwell by the shoulders. The ape raises the man and tosses him into a stack of film cans, which skid and clatter, almost drowning out the loud crack of Cromwell's head hitting the iron base of the overturned Klieg light.

I watch dully as the gorilla's head slides back to expose the sweat-drenched face of Ray Corrigan. Then a dark red liquid seems to ooze down over the lens of my camera eye and it's fade to black.

* * * *

I come out of a bad sleep with a raging headache, into the fresh air.

"I'm never wearing that thing again," Ray says with satisfaction. "And I'm never buckling under studio pressure again either. I'll tell the world." He had finished with a screen test for a new version of "The Lost World" at 20th Century Fox when he'd interrupted my dance with Cromwell and had him escorted off the site. I realize that the studio fixer probably won't ever be charged with abducting Chandler's body or even blackmailing Garner, but I promise to myself that I'll get him on an assault charge.

While Corrigan climbs out of his monkey suit, I thank him again for saving my butt. We're seated in his office at the back of the saloon. "I felt bad when I learned that Cromwell had taken the body away, but I didn't want any more trouble." He shrugs into a new western outfit; this one includes a gray shirt with snap-button pockets big enough to hold paperback novels. "So now are you going to tell me why Garner didn't show up for shooting here? Browne was complaining earlier that he had to re-write the 'Iron Hand' script to replace your client with Jack Kelly."

The elder cowpoke and I ambled together past a stage coach drawn up in front of the Silver Dollar saloon. I've changed back into my dry clothes, intending to leave the Wild West behind, but I guess Corrigan has earned an answer to his question about the actor's absence.

"It's no big secret." I watch a dust-covered hombre wrangle a group of tumbleweeds down the street. "Garner's tied up for a week in a hospital."

"Sick?"

"They're testing his blood. He told me he has a rare type and his agent's son will die without it."

"And you believe him?"

"Yes. I do. So, they need him to rest and eat and then they draw a pint or two every few days."

"Ugh! But yeah, that sounds like Jim, after all. I hear he'll go out on strike against the studio, if SAG follows the WGA's lead. Maybe I will, too. I guess it's good to stand your ground on principle."

"Helps you sleep at night, too."

The mayor of Corriganville waves to me from in front of the fake Chinese laundry.

I wave back and drive off into the lemon sunset, listening to "Running Bear" on the car radio.

* * * *

The Ventura County cops never did find the gun or Christine Chandler's body. She lies asleep, I guess, buried somewhere in the hills under western skies. Or maybe she's weighted down in Corriganville's manmade lake where they shot the underwater scenes of the Black Lagoon creature back in 1954. In a way it doesn't matter, since she had no family that anyone knew of. Just a nobody.

At the back of my mind, I can't shake the feeling that I've simply been a catalyst for events again; that my nosing around has caused other individuals to act against their better nature. Ask enough questions and things happen. Kick enough sleeping dogs and someone gets bit. One more wicked image to trouble my sleep.

Like I say, I don't enjoy pain. It's just part of the cost of doing business. And I swear to God, my business with Mr. Steve Cromwell is far from over, fella.

John Hegenberger is the author of 14 books in the last three years. His Stan Wade, L.A. PI novel, *Spyfall*, won a Silver Falchion award. His latest novel, *Tripleye*, came out in June. He has an international thriller, *The Pandora Block*, due out February 2018.

DON'T MISS OUR NEXT ISSUE!

Sure, you can try to keep the *Cat* coming to your house by putting out a saucer of milk every night. But for guaranteed copies, your best bet is a subscription. For the next 4 issues, send your check/money order/bearer bonds for $39.99 to:

Wildside Press LLC
7945 MacArthur Blvd., Suite 215
Cabin John, MD 20818

or subscribe online at one of our web sites:

bcmystery.com
The online home of the Black Cat Mystery Community! (There's lots more than just our magazine, including free mystery ebooks, writer's guidelines, forums, etc.)

wildsidepress.com
The main Wildside Press site, with all of our books and magazines.

GUIDELINES

We are happy to read author submissions, but only during open submission periods. Visit the Wildside Press Facebook page or our web site, bcmystery.com, for announcements. We regret that due to time constraints, stories received outside of open submission periods cannot be read.

THE SECOND MRS. PORTER
Melba Marlett

INTRODUCTION

Melba Marlett (1909-1994) is an unjustly obscure mystery novelist, short story writer, playwright, and essayist. Her most famous story is probably "The Second Mrs. Porter," which appeared in *Alfred Hitchcock's Mystery Magazine* in November, 1986. Her novels—which Wildside Press is set to reissue in 2018—include *Death Has a Thousand Doors* (1941), *The Devil Builds a Chapel* (1942), *Escape While I Can* (1944), *Tomorrow Will Be Monday* (1946), and *Death Is In the Garden* (1951).

*

She opened her eyes and didn't know where she was. The word "orientation" swam into her mind. "That's it," she thought. "I am very, very comfortable, but I am not oriented." The shortcoming did not seem important to her. She was wrapped in a beautiful peace, a consciousness of well-being that was intoxicating. The light blue robe that invested her shoulders, the delicately striped afghan that covered her knees were airy miracles; the narrow hands that lay in her lap were smooth and pink-tipped. She flexed them, enjoying the smooth response of the muscles. "What wonderful hands," she thought, surprised, pleased. They were as strange to her as everything else.

Drowsily she studied the handsome room. It seemed to be a kind of bed-sitting room, furnished in muted blues and greens, with everything precisely placed. Her eyes traversed it slowly, lingering on the pretty bed against the far wall, on the enchanting little boudoir chair, on the bowl of ruffled white flowers—were they sweet peas?—was there a flower called that?—on the low table, on the mirror whose reflection doubled the size of the room and showed her a woman in a light blue robe, lying on a chaise longue by a wide window. She knew at once that she was looking at herself, but she had no feelings of recognition, nor any great interest in the matter. She turned her head, without raising it, toward the window.

Through the thin white curtain she looked at a wide green lawn, enliv- ened with petunia beds, marked with tall accents of cypress and oak. The sunshine had a late-afternoon slant to it. Odd to have bars on a window that gave on such a handsome view.

When she woke again, it was evening, and she was in bed. Across the room, in lamplight now, she saw the chaise longue, the afghan neatly folded at its foot. A woman dressed in white was stacking dishes on a tray, her back to the bed.

Her mind supplied the word she should use. "Nurse," she said.

The woman turned around so sharply that the dishes clattered. Then her face smoothed and she approached the bed. "Well, Mrs. Porter," she said. "I'm glad you're so much better this evening. Is there anything I can get for you?"

She had a feeling that she should be very careful. The dishes gave her an inspiration. "I'm hungry," she said.

"I'm not surprised. You had very little supper. What would you like?"

Of course, she had not had supper at all. She would have remembered eating supper. Careful, careful. "Some ice cream? Perhaps some tea?" She hadn't the faintest notion of what either thing was. They were only words that had come into her head.

The nurse smiled and picked up the tray. "I'll bring them right away." The door swished shut behind her.

She wanted nothing more than to stay right where she was and enjoy the room in solitude, but she had a presentiment of trickery that made her slide from the bed and circle the room, looking for—well, anything that would give her an advantage in the guessing game. They were trying to make her believe she was in a hospital, though this room, with its bars at the windows, was not like her concept of hospital. (Funny how she knew some things without knowing how she knew them. It was the important things she *didn't* know that she must discover.) They wanted her to think she was sick, though there could not be another person on earth who had such a feeling of health. They said she was Mrs. Porter, but she didn't recognize the name.

As if on command she opened a dresser drawer and it was full of letters. They were addressed to Mrs. Robert W. Porter, Women's Memo- rial Hospital, and each one had been neatly slit open, its contents not so neatly put back. (She nearly laughed. I suppose they'll try to tell me I've read every one, she thought.) Quickly she slid several of them out of their envelopes, just far enough to see the opening lines. "Dear Ellen," they began. And "Darling Ellen" and "My poor Ellen." The dates ranged wildly through different months of different years. She put them back precisely and closed the drawer. If this was part of the scheme to convince her that she was Mrs. Porter, what a lot of trouble they had gone to, with those variegated scripts and writing papers. I suppose there is a Mrs. Porter somewhere, she thought, climbing back into bed.

The minute she saw the tray, she recognized both ice cream and tea (how could she have forgotten?) and began to consume them, daintily, to make them last longer. Their deliciousness absorbed her completely, as if they were the first food she had ever eaten.

When she looked up, a tall man in a gray suit was standing beside the nurse.

"I'm your doctor," he said. "Dr. Lindsay. Remember me?"

"Yes," she said, falsely. "How are you?"

"The point is, how are *you?* Mrs. O'Hara called me and I came right down. What about your vision? Can you see me quite clearly?"

If you only knew, she thought—how *very* clearly I can see you, with the excitement in your eyes and voice and the significant little looks you and Mrs. O'Hara are exchanging. "Certainly," she said.

"No blurring? No double vision?" He took a small silver tube from his pocket. "I'm going to shine this little light in your eyes. It'll take only a few minutes. It won't hurt you."

The light shining into one eye did not preclude the vision of the other. Through it, she studied the texture of his skin and guessed his age to be forty. Younger than herself; the woman she had seen in the mirror must be at least forty-five. "You have reddish whiskers, Dr. Lindsay," she said.

He snapped off the light and stepped back. "Haven't shaved since this morning. Do you know your name?"

"My name is Ellen Porter," she said. "I'm in Women's Memorial Hospital. I think I have been here for a long time." It was the right thing to have said. She heard the intake of his breath.

"And Mrs. O'Hara, here. Do you know her?"

Something hinged on this answer. The electricity in the room tingled along her nerves. "I'm sorry," she said. "I don't know Mrs. O'Hara."

"Of course you don't," he said, triumphantly. "She's brand new. Just came on this evening." He turned to the nurse. "Well, Mrs. O'Hara, you're a miracle worker. Now if you two girls will just settle down for tonight, I'll see Mrs. Porter the first thing in the morning. The nurses have been telling me that they find that chaise comfortable for napping, and I don't believe Mrs. Porter will be requiring much attention."

It was time to take a giant step. "I won't be requiring anything at all tonight," Ellen said. "Is there any other place where Mrs. O'Hara could sleep?" She made appealing gestures against their consternation. "It seems to be that I've been with people forever. It would be so—normal, to have my room to myself."

The word "normal" turned the tide. Yes, Mrs. O'Hara could be elsewhere, close at hand, for frequent checks. The night light in the bathroom could be left on. And yes, certainly, she could have more ice cream for breakfast. The request pleased them inordinately. They went away smiling.

Most of that night she spent in the bathroom, reading the letters from the drawer, one by one under the night light, with the bathroom door closed. Periodically she returned to her bed, to act the perfectly sleeping patient. If Mrs. O'Hara did surprise her, it would be in a normal situation, and she would at once flush the letter away. But Mrs. O'Hara came at only the right intervals.

By the time her table clock said three, she was back in bed, thinking hard about Ellen Porter. The woman was incomprehensible to her, to anyone with common sense. Mrs. Porter, it seemed, was a woman of great wealth who spent her time in litigation and in giving offense. Her husband, Robert, from whom she had been estranged—no mention of divorce, however—had been injured in an automobile accident. Her remaining family consisted of some distant cousins, who appeared to have hopes of becoming her heirs. There were references to the unsatisfactory behavior of a Mr. Arthur Crandall, who was Mrs. Porter's attorney and made of the same kind of stone as she was. Over and over the letters said, "You have so much, we have so little." Sue's education—therapy for Tony—subsistence for an aging great-aunt. Small requests, really, to make of a woman who had millions. Most expressed a perfunctory hope for her better health, but one, signed Gregory Porter, was belligerent: "You can hide in that hospital till Hell freezes over, but we'll get you into court the minute you leave. You have never fulfilled your father's promises to us, though we signed those papers on the strength of them and in good faith. Robert says that he is willing to settle, but that he can't prevail upon you. Five years, or ten, the going gets tougher, but we can wait. How does it feel to know that so many people wish you were dead?"

Well, Mrs. Porter *was* dead, or would they have dared to give her name to a stranger? (If only I knew my real name, she thought, I suppose it's some medicine they give me.) But Mrs. Porter must also be made to seem alive for some reason, so a conspiracy was being engineered to that end, and somehow she had become involved in it, an empty-headed puppet on God-knew-whose strings. I have to play along, she thought, because I don't know what else to do; but somewhere along the way I'll escape them, if I'm very patient and very clever.

The game was to learn from them while they thought they were learning from her, and she found it easy for two reasons. First, Dr. Lindsay and the staff seemed to want her to set her own pace in "remembering," as they called it; and, second, her senses remained magnificently acute, so that in the faces and voices of the people around her she caught the smallest and most fleeting changes. Watching their souls move behind their eyes gave her the clues to what they wanted her to say.

She learned to be bold on occasion. "Why don't I have visitors?" she asked Dr. Lindsay after a month of their daily interviews. "I should think that Mr. Crandall might have come by now. Or Robert."

Plain as day was the astonishment behind the professional mask. "Do you *want* to see your husband?"

"Of course," she said, promptly. "I realize that we weren't on the best of terms, but still—has he recovered from the accident?"

The jolt of that threw him against the back of his chair, but he kept his voice calm. "Yes, he's recovered. What do you remember about—the accident?"

"Nothing, really. Only that there was one. When did it happen?"

"Five years ago."

"As long as that?" She rubbed her forehead so that she could study him between her fingers. "Was I—in it? Is that what brought me here?"

His face was all confirmation, though he averted his eyes. "Don't worry about it. You're coming along so well. No use to force these things. That's why we're not allowing you visitors until a little later."

She smiled at him. "That makes me feel better. I know I wasn't one of the world's most popular women, but I did think somebody ought to come by."

"They'll come as soon as we let them."

"And write as soon as you let them?"

He made a note on the chart before him. "I have no objection to letters. We screen them, you see, so if there's anything too troublesome, we can protect you from it."

"Oh. You read them first?"

"Yes. Every letter that comes in is pre-read by staff. Don't mind the inked-out sections. They're for your own good." But—there had been no inked-out sections at all in the neatly-opened letters she had read that first night and which, without notice or explanation, had disappeared from the dresser drawer by the next time she opened it. Had they decided those letters were a mistake? And how could they let her have visitors when the very first one would see that the woman who was supposed to be Ellen Porter was really no such person?

Serious as her predicament might be, she found she could not worry about it with any consistency. Life was marvelously pleasant, now that she was "fully ambulatory." The private nurses, with their professional nosiness, were removed; and, with the coming of Wally West, she was given the beatific freedom of the hospital grounds.

Wally was a tall, spidery eighteen-year-old with a shimmering mind and the composure of a saint. He was a senior at the high school in Northfield, the little town whose church steeples were visible down in the valley, and he was employed by the hospital, late afternoons, as a Walker.

"More like a Tagger-Alonger," Wally said. "You just walk where you want to, and I tag along. If you want to talk, we talk. If you don't want to, I keep quiet. The thing is, don't worry about talking. I always have plenty to think about."

At first she was content just to walk, miles a day, over the meadows and woodland that belonged to the hospital. Then Wally began to insist that she sit down every now and then.

"Dr. Lindsay says you're losing too much weight," he said. "Let's sit on this bench and watch the squirrels."

"And talk," she said, agreeably.

"Okay. But I better tell you that the doctor gets a written report from me about you, once a week. I have an agreement with him that I can tell my patients that. Don't want to go around feeling like a Judas or something."

"That's all right. I have nothing to hide."

"I told 'em that already. I said to Dr. Lindsay, 'Mrs. Porter's getting so well, she doesn't need me.' But he says to keep on anyway."

"And I say so, too." The October air was marvelous, and she raised her face to it. "I don't *feel* ill, you know. I'm not even sure what's supposed to be wrong with me."

"Well, plenty *was*. When I first came to work here, more than a year ago, they told me they'd inherited you from some other hospital. You were just a bundle in a chair—you know, like a vegetable—didn't talk or see or hear. The nurses got you up and dressed you, and walked you, and put you to bed again, and you weren't *with* it. Now, well, you're a miracle. You don't even look like yourself. I'd never recognize you as the same woman."

"Did you see me close up, Wally? Did you come right up and look into my face? Surely I'd remember that."

"No, I just saw you from a distance, being trundled around. You looked like this." He slid down limply on the bench, pushed his hair over his eyes, let his head and jaw go slack. "Strictly nobody home. The sickest person in the whole hospital." He slid upright again. "I wrote a composition about you for my English class. Didn't use your name, of course, that wouldn't have been right. I called it 'The Woman Who Went Away.' Got an A on it, too."

"I'd like to read it. Could I?"

"If Dr. Lindsay says so. I'll ask him."

"Don't." The word was too impulsive and she hastened to lighten it. "It's good policy to let sleeping doctors lie."

"I couldn't let you see it without his permission, Mrs. Porter. Something in it might set you back, it takes a psychiatrist to know."

She reached over and patted his hand. "That's all right, Wally. Don't worry about it."

By September, she knew every path and twig on the hospital's back acreage. Her favorite spot was a little curving abandoned garden, where re-seeded pansies and poppies struggled with a heavy invasion of weeds. "Wonder why they let this go?" she said to Wally. "It must have been very pretty once, and you can see half the country from up here."

"What I like about it is that it has *benches.* What do you say we sit for a few minutes?"

"You sit, and I'll—I'll *weed.*"

It was a happy inspiration. Besides the kneeling and pulling that stretched her muscles and warmed her blood, there was the pleasure of seeing a design unfold. Here there had been a big clump of bleeding-heart, and here had been—was it foxglove? And over everything were the weeds, vigorous and furiously stubborn.

Day after day she struggled with them, panting with determination. Some had surface roots and came away easily, but, if she didn't get every scrap of them, they regrew, almost overnight. Others had roots that went down a foot, and all of them reappeared at a moment's notice.

"I'm getting to be an expert on weeds," she said to Wally. "They're fascinating in a curious kind of way. Sometimes I dream about them at night. Sort of a nightmare, where I keep pulling and pulling, and the weeds just stay as thick as ever! I wish I had a book about them. Maybe there's one in the hospital library."

"Well, you're making an impression here," said Wally, grinning. "Only three weeks' work and you've cleared a space at least two feet square. Did you always like to garden?"

"Yes," she said, firmly, wondering if it were true.

"Then maybe you have some gardening books at home, and Dr. Lindsay could have them brought for you."

"Of course," she said, smoothly. "I wonder why I didn't think of that myself. You know, next Monday I'm going to start right in the middle there, where it's thickest. Maybe, just maybe, it was planted in a clock pattern, and the middle ought to tell me."

The very next day, at their morning session, she broached the subject to Dr. Lindsay. "Are there any books about weeds? I'd like some."

"Wally says you're really going after them. I've been asking around, and nobody seems to know anything about your weeded-over garden. Must have been part of the original planting, forty years ago. It might show up on an old landscaping map, if I could find one." He had noticed her hands, and he was shocked. "My God, Mrs. Porter, the least you can do is wear gloves when you go digging! I can't have people thinking you take care of our grounds single-handed! And, yes, I'll see that you get some gardening books."

"I need some different clothes, too," she said. "Nothing in my closet really fits me anymore. I'm a different shape than I used to be. My waist-line's the same, but I'm rounder above and below it."

"We'll get one of the nurses to take you down to the village to shop—and maybe to help you research weeds in the Carnegie library there. How will that suit you?" He leaned across and handed her a typewritten page. "This is from Mr. Crandall, came yesterday. It's not much more than a re-quest to come and see you." His eyes were so intent upon her that she had to look away to keep from laughing. "I'm going to have to let him come, I suppose. He's a member of the trust that's been handling your affairs while you've been with us."

"I know that he's my lawyer," she said, casually. "I didn't know about the trust." She folded the letter and put it back on his desk. "Is Robert a member of the trust, too?"

"I don't think so. Perhaps they ask his advice, I wouldn't know. Con-sidering that the two of you weren't on good enough terms at the time of the accident to be living together, the court decided to—"

"If we weren't living together, how did we come to be in that car together?"

"That's what the police wanted to know. There was quite an investiga-tion, particularly when it looked as if you weren't going to live. But then you began to recover—"

She laughed. "A vegetable in a chair! How encouraged they all must have been!"

"Believe me, Mrs. Porter, it took medical miracles to get you even as far as the vegetable stage." He leaned back in his chair and smiled at her. "Don't bother to pretend that you remember anything from that earlier period. There was neurological damage that had to be repaired. You could not possibly recall anything from that first six months after the accident."

She tried to look prettily indignant. "Pretend? Why should I pretend?"

"I'm not sure. I have the feeling, off and on, that you're playing games with me. Please don't do it."

And I have the feeling that you're playing games with me, she thought swiftly, and that the name of today's little game is Get Her to Confide in You. "Dear Dr. Lindsay," she said, appealingly, "it's only that I like to please you. I'm not treacherous, only feminine. Sometimes I think I know what you want me to say, so I say it!"

"Whether it's true or not?"

"Well, after I say it, it always *seems* true."

He shook his head. "We'll never get you put back together that way."

"I'm not sure I want to be put back together," she said, daringly. "I wasn't as nice a person then as I am now."

That surprised him, but he rallied. "'Healthy' and 'nice' aren't always the same thing, Mrs. Porter, and it's 'healthy' we're trying for. The more honest you try to be, the more quickly I can let you leave here."

The leap of hope in her heart surprised her by its strength. "Should I want to leave here?"

"Yes."

"And I'm not healthy enough now?"

"No. There's something—well, I'm not satisfied with your adjustment. You've been through a dreadful ordeal—pain, surgery, a long invalidism, partial rebuilding of your face, loss of memory—and none of it seems to have touched you at all. This indicates a lack of realization that is, well, worrisome."

For the first time she was convinced that he was a completely honest man, and she nearly told him the whole story. How Ellen Porter must be dead or in hiding, and that she (infuriatingly nameless) had somehow been substituted, and that no one had supposed she would recover enough (from whatever had been done to her) to know the difference, but that somehow she had. And, just as swiftly, she saw that it would be wrong to involve this young doctor by alerting him. As long as they both appeared innocent and unaware, they would be safe, she was sure of it.

She ventured one cautious question. "This is not the first hospital I've been in, is it, and you're not the original doctor to take my case?"

"No. There were three—maybe four, I can look it up—other hospitals, and, as for doctors—" he threw up his hands "—I must be the thousandth. Someday I'll show you your medical file. It's a foot thick. By the time you were turned over to us, everybody thought that you were merely custodial, you see. Then you surprised us by getting better, and I began to cherish the hope of a complete cure. Unfortunately, in a case like yours, it's the patient who has to do most of the work, and all you've demonstrated is a disposition to avoid the effort."

"I won't pretend any more," she said, smiling at him with genuine affection, but, of course, it was a promise she could not possibly keep.

That interview marked the end of her comfortable isolation. She had known there were other patients in the hospital, hundreds of them she was told, but she had seen nothing of them except at a distance. Her quarters were in a small wing of the building that was restricted, apparently, to her own use. They included her large room and bath, a small kitchen where trays were left for distribution elsewhere on the floor, the offices of Dr. Lindsay and his secretary, and an elegant meeting room labeled Hospital Board that, as far as she had observed, never had a meeting in it. It was a marvel that so busy an institution should have so quiet a corner. Every afternoon and evening, from her window she saw the cars, creeping up the long and distant drive from the main road (which she had never seen) to fill the two large parking lots; and, at ten o'clock at night, there might still be the car lights of a departing late visitor. Yet all day long, up to now, she had spoken to no one but Dr. Lindsay, a floor nurse or two, and Wally. Now she was going to be put through a period of social testing, and she must be doubly on guard.

The shopping trip to the village was easy. The stores were good, her accounts limited only by the number of times she wished to sign her name—which she was careful to do in a schoolbookish hand that had no distinguishing marks, she hadn't the slightest notion of what Ellen Porter's signature should be like—and her mentor, a young nurse's aide named Miss Raymond, pleasant and only mildly watchful. But oh, the exhilaration of being outside again, of becoming, for a few hours, one of the everyday inhabitants of the everyday world! From where they were walking on Main Street, she could see the depot set on the edge of the town and the tracks fanning out from it, and, for a wild minute, she estimated the number of blocks she would have to run to reach it and her possible rate of speed, as matched against Miss Raymond's. She reproved herself immediately for such silliness. If she escaped that way, they would search the world over for her until they found her and brought her back to her luxurious jail. The only good way to leave was with their full connivance and approval, which she must earn by showing them *(who?)* that she was perfectly willing to play the role they had assigned her.

Even this knowledge could not keep her from savoring the day—October's blue and gold, the leaf smoke, the calling of children to each other in school play yards, the good lunch at the little restaurant on the square where the marble Civil War soldier stood holding his rifle, the lovely things they showed her in the stores. She bought presents for the nurses and huge boxes of candy for the clerical help; serviceable skirts and sweaters, but in pretty colors, for herself; a bottle of perfume for Miss Raymond; a bright jacket for Wally; a handsome leather box for Dr. Lindsay's desk; and, on impulse, a round glass paperweight that responded to the light by throwing back a hundred different shades of blue.

Miss Raymond said the paperweight was the prettiest thing she had ever seen. "A person could look at it forever, Mrs. Porter. Is it for your little desk by the window?"

"No, it's not for myself at all. It's for Robert." It came out so easily that it must have been in her mind from the beginning, yet she would take an oath that she had never contemplated giving Robert a gift, nor even considered the prospect of meeting him. "He's—he's my husband."

"Yes, I know, and he ought to be awfully pleased. Well, shall we go find your books?"

Across the street, granite steps led up to a door marked Carnegie Public Library, where, undoubtedly, there were reference books that would tell her all about the very rich Ellen Porter. "Miss Raymond, if you have some shopping of your own to do, I promise to stay in the reading room till you come back. Why don't you—"

"No, indeed, Mrs. Porter. I'm not going to leave you for a moment."

"I only want to see some gardening books. I want to read about weeds."

"Gardening books are all right," said Miss Raymond, "if you show me the titles of what you read, and if I'm sitting right beside you." She had the grace to look apologetic. "Your reading is still controlled, you see. Dr. Lindsay's orders."

"Oh, dear, just when I felt so free! Come along, then, and tell the librarian what I can look at."

The librarian said they had no books on weeds, only some government pamphlets, but any book on gardens was bound to mention weeds, it seemed to her, and Miss Raymond concurred. So gardening books were heaped on the table in front of Mrs. Porter, and she turned the pages resignedly, while her nurse became immediately absorbed in fashion magazines.

But luck was with her. The third book she opened was entitled *Famous Gardens of the World,* and Chapter Ten was headed "Mrs. Robert Porter's Garden at Quercorum in Connecticut"! It was illustrated by a full-page picture, in color, of Mrs. Porter, standing near her prize delphinium, with a great white stone house stretching away behind her. Her heart began to beat suffocatingly, but she controlled her breath and composed her face. Both the pictured woman and the house were completely strange to her.

Greedily she assimilated what information she could. Ellen Porter had married her second cousin, Robert Porter, more than twenty years ago. The marriage was childless but the void had been filled with the diversions of the wealthy—travel, the maintenance of six residences (only the one in Connecticut was identified), yachting, the breeding of race horses, the exchanges of visits with friends. Mrs. Porter looked after her own business affairs. "It was my branch of the family that made the money," she was quoted as saying, "and I feel it my responsibility to look after it. Robert is really not a businessman so it all works out for the best."

She studied the picture for a long time. The real Ellen Porter was at least fifteen years older than herself, with a high-bridged nose, deep frown lines, a tight straight-lipped mouth. The conspirators had been careful about the only two characteristics that plastic surgery could not change; height and eye color. "So I'm tall, and my eyes are blue," she mused, "but where did they find me? When was the substitution made? Whatever my real identity, I must have had friends, relatives. But I suppose they wouldn't recognize me now, anyway." She smoothed her hair, feeling the tiny scars hidden there. "So there can be no danger to anyone, as long as my memory doesn't return, completely—and with all that surgery, I bet they've made sure that it won't."

Then she turned the page and saw the picture labeled "Robert Porter." How long she stared at it, she had no idea. When she raised her eyes, Miss Raymond was still reading her magazines, the librarian was helping some teenagers with the card catalogue, all was as it had been. Except that now she was in love with Robert Porter, who must be one of the handsomest and most appealing men in existence.

Alive with plans that would bring Robert to her, she was politic with Dr. Lindsay the next morning and spoke casually about Mr. Crandall's eventual visit.

"What if I want to make changes in my business affairs, Dr. Lindsay. Am I allowed to? I mean, is my signature legal?"

"It will be, the minute I vouch for it, Mrs. Porter. I'm not ready to do that, yet. Mr. Crandall has your power-of-attorney, however, and I daresay he'll be inclined to act on your suggestions."

She smiled at him. "You don't consider me sane?"

"'Sane' is a word I rarely use. I just think you're not—ready."

And that afternoon, as if to corroborate him, came the relapse, shockingly, suddenly, out of the blue. One minute she was weeding in the very middle of the Hidden Garden, calling occasional remarks to Wally on his bench; the next, she was staring down at something smooth and hard that her fingers were encountering, under the mat of weeds. It was a metal plate, brass it seemed, and as she tore the weeds away, she saw the writing on it. "To the memory of—" it began. She scraped and pulled, deliberately averting her eyes until she could see it all. "To the memory of Ellen Porter, 1900-1962, this garden, of her own planning, is gratefully dedicated." Streaked with dirt, panting from exertion, she stared at it, openmouthed. So Ellen Porter was dead, and this is where they had buried her.

A black cloud of terror swept down on her, suffocating, paralyzing. She fought it off, got to her feet, ran—somewhere, anywhere. She heard Wally's voice calling to her, but she could not stop. She collapsed, finally, against the wall of the hospital, near the side door that they always used, and felt Wally's grasp on her arms.

"Mrs. Porter, what's happened? Are you all right? Mrs. Porter?"

She saw a nurse and an orderly racing up behind him. "Yes," she managed to gasp, "I'm—all right. Saw—a snake. Always—been—scared to death—of snakes."

"Good grief! I think you just set a new world's record for the half-mile." He turned to the newcomers. "She saw a snake." But the staff was suspicious, alert. They put her to bed for the rest of the day, had the private nurses back again for forty-eight hours, chatted amiably to her—and watched. Dr. Lindsay paid her a special visit. "Seems funny to see you in bed again," he said. "Just a precaution against your having overdone it."

"It was a silly way to act. I feel so apologetic."

"We went up to look for your snake, but we didn't find one." He took her wrist between his fingers. "That seems to be a pretty little garden you've unearthed. We're going to ask the hospital board to let us restore it. It shouldn't have been let go." He put her hand down on the coverlet and patted it. "Must have been a shock to you, coming across your own name like that. It was your Aunt Ellen, you know, who gave us this hospital."

"I'd—forgotten."

"No ingratitude involved on our part, just a shortage of gardeners during the war. It's only a memorial kind of thing. Your aunt is buried in Rome, I believe."

She could not keep her voice from sounding defensive. "It did look like a grave, you know."

"And who did you think was buried there?" he asked gently.

Her thoughts ran around like mice in a cage, while the silence grew and grew. "I—I don't believe I thought at all," she said, finally. "It was—how does Wally say it?—a gut reaction."

"Is that your best analysis? I can't quite believe that, Mrs. Porter."

"Then work on it till you can!" she said, crossly. "Some things aren't easy!" In his shout of surprised laughter her tension eased. "And you can just take that night nurse out of my room tonight, too. I can't sleep with another person in the room—unless it's Robert." The last three words amazed her—she had not meant to say them—but she realized that they were absolutely right. *"When* are you going to let Robert come?" she asked, and burst into tears.

"Mr. Crandall can come week after next," he said, "and Robert a week or so after that." He handed her a handkerchief. "That's rushing things, but if you refuse to be patient and rational—"

"I have been *extremely* patient, Dr. Lindsay."

"And rational?"

She smiled at him, while she wiped her eyes. "Women aren't supposed to be rational. Ask anybody."

He went away laughing, and the dangerous moment was past. Heavens, he was such a young man, hard to mislead, but not difficult to charm!

That night she received the first of the shocking notes.

She had fallen asleep reading, her bed light on. When she awoke, the door to her room was swinging slightly, and she called, "Come back. I'm awake." But no one came, and she guessed that the draft had been caused by the opening of an outside door in some distant corridor. It had happened before, on windy evenings.

Then she turned to put her book on the bedside table, and there lay the note. It was on plain white paper—torn from her own tablet, she thought later—folded once, handwritten in large, jagged, black letters.

> Insist on Robert's coming to see you. Be sure to mention the Gregory Porter lawsuit to Arthur Crandall, beforehand. Robert always wanted that settled.
> E.

She lay motionless for a long time before she could summon the nerve to re-read it. Not once did she doubt that it was from the real Ellen Porter; the positiveness of the words and the insolence of the ugly handwriting were absolutely convincing. She was glad to put a match to it, to see it fall into black flakes in the ashtray.

It cost her a real effort to turn off the light, though leaving it on would, she knew, eventually bring nurses to ask questions. For hours she lay awake, ears strained for any hint of approach, but there were only the usual hospital night sounds, hushed, as always in this isolated room. In the first dim light of morning, she reached for her pen and wrote a note of her own.

Dear Mrs. Porter:

I want to cooperate, but I don't understand my situation. Now that you are well enough to get around, I don't see why I am needed any more at all. Is there any place where we could meet and talk? I am very willing to be helpful—it's the only way I know to get out of here—but I could do much better if I knew what was expected of me.

She could not decide on a signature, so she simply folded the note and left it where the other had been.

Ten minutes later, she sat up suddenly, tore the note into tiny shreds, and burned it, too, though her hands were shaking so badly she had trouble holding the match. Oh, that was all she needed, to have someone come across a communication like that one! "Crazy," they'd say. "A crazy woman writing formal letters to herself!" Nor could she go roaming over the hospital, snooping and trying doors.

She must preserve an effect of normality; she dared do nothing else. Any future communication had to depend on the real Mrs. Porter, who, startlingly enough, did not seem unfriendly. And was, at least, alive.

* * * *

Arthur Crandall turned out to be a gray-haired, stocky, bustling man, with the alert, sidewise glance of a high class horse that has been mistreated. "You're looking well, Mrs. Porter," he said. "Glad to see you so blooming."

"Be honest," she said. "Would you have known me if you'd passed me on the street?"

"Well, maybe not. But the change is all to the good. All to the good. There are many resemblances, naturally. I think I'd know your hands anywhere." He sat down opposite her. "Now, what can I do for you, after all this long while? What's on your mind?"

"Several things. The first is that, since I'm healthy once more, I'd like to leave the hospital."

"That depends entirely on Dr. Lindsay. He's the one who has to discharge you. Naturally we'd be happy to see him do it. There are matters on which we'd welcome your decision."

"I hope you'll say so to him. He won't discuss my leaving with me at all."

"That's because he still has some reservations about you. He didn't tell me what they were. Just said that he had 'em. Medical men are pretty conservative, you know. Have to give them a little time." He slapped his hand down on the arm of his chair. "But if you could see yourself, sitting there, smiling, with pink in your face—you look better this minute than you ever did in your whole life! And I've known you for forty years!"

She smiled her best smile at him. "Thank you, Arthur." A small tremor in his face told her that the first-name basis was new. "I'm very fond of Dr. Lindsay, but you're going to have to find some little ways to pressure him into letting me go. Not bad little ways. Nice little ways. I remember you as a subtle man, Arthur."

He flushed with pleasure. "Oh, I think we can hurry him up a little. Surely by early spring we'll have brought him around. Will that suit you?"

"Yes. You understand that there are things I will never remember because of the surgery. Dr. Lindsay says there's no help for that."

"I understand. Everyone on the board understands."

"Good. Now the next item is Robert. Will he come to visit me? I imagine that he isn't very eager to see me, but I want very much to see him."

"So I was told. Yes, I believe that he'll come. For one thing he's still legally your husband. For another, he isn't a man to hold grudges." He cleared his throat. "As your lawyer I'd be interested in knowing *why* you want to see him."

She spoke simply and directly. "I want to be reconciled to him, if he'll have me."

"My God!" he said. "Mrs. Porter, are you sure? After all those years of our dragging him into court on one contrived pretext or another? I don't think I'll be able to look him in the face, much less talk to him!"

"I'll take all the blame—for everything," she said earnestly, "and you're going to have to help me convince him that I've changed. For instance, settle the Gregory Porter business right away. Give Gregory what he wants, give him more than he wants. It's long overdue."

Mr. Crandall's jaw went slack. "But that would mean—mind you, I've always been in favor of settling with Gregory, all we could do was delay him, he was always going to win in the long run—but to settle now, and willingly, knocks the props out of our defense against the suits of about eight other relatives of yours who think they're entitled to—"

"Settle with them, too. I want them off my mind."

"*All* of them?"

"All of them. As the old proverb has it, 'There are no pockets in shrouds.'"

"Well, of course, that's an eminently sensible viewpoint, Mrs. Porter, and, as you'll see when we go over the figures, your finances have never been in better shape. You can afford it."

She smiled. "What I don't want to afford is the time to go over the figures. I'm going to be completely honest with you, Arthur. If Robert will have me back, I intend to give my power-of-attorney to him and turn over the whole boring business to the two of you."

"But—but what will *you* be doing?"

"Enjoying life," she said.

He made gasping sounds for ten minutes, but, in the long run, she thought he was not displeased. She made bold to kiss his cheek before he left. "Dear Arthur, you've put up with so much. Just a few months more and I hope you'll be dealing with a stable Robert instead of an eccentric Ellen."

He was nonplussed, but he was a man who said what he had on his mind. "If you're not sane right this minute, Mrs. Porter, then there's no hope for any of us."

* * * *

So she had made the right impression on the very important Mr. Crandall, and the results began to appear immediately. The hospital people, always attentive and kind, snapped into something like military precision, and Dr. Lindsay, though friendly as usual, began to look harried. "I've told your Mr. Crandall that he can begin to familiarize you with your business affairs, though I think he's being a bit premature. Don't let him tire you out."

"I won't. Though I don't believe I'll ever be very interested in business things again. I told him I wanted Robert to take care of all that for me."

"I think I should tell you that Robert is not being responsive to the idea of a reconciliation," he said, frowning. "Like Mr. Crandall, I think that he'll come 'round eventually, but I don't want you to build on it and then be disappointed."

She quoted him to himself. "'I will face reality as honestly and cheerfully as possible.'"

"Good. Plus a touch of rule five."

"'I will assume that the unhappy are always wrong.' Therefore, I will try to be happy."

"I thought you *were*, you know. Now it seems that you can't wait to get away from us."

"Please, please don't think that, Dr. Lindsay. It's not that I'm running away from something, it's that I'm running *toward* something else."

His face cleared. "Well, that helps. Now, let's get down to work. Nurse Hanson tells me she's found you sleeping with your lights on three times this week. How do you account for that? Does darkness worry you all of a sudden?"

* * * *

Every Tuesday afternoon, like clockwork, Mr. Crandall visited her, with eyes that saw everything. "New dress, Mrs. Porter? Beautiful shade of blue. Your sapphires might go well with that." And the next day a messenger from the bank appeared in an armored car with case after case of extravagant blue baubles.

Embarrassed at the display, she chose sparingly and sent the rest back. "We have no security precautions here, Arthur, and I didn't like to risk—but aren't these earrings sublime? Are they really real?"

"Yes. We have a good many facsimiles, but those are the real thing. I have a theory that it does jewels good to have a lovely woman wear them."

"Thank you. It would be nice to be younger."

"You were not nearly as handsome then as you are now."

"Will Robert think so?"

His mouth tightened. "It has been some time since Robert has favored me with his opinions, Mrs. Porter."

Most of the time, however, it was like having one's own personal genie. One shiver from Ellen-in-a-wool-coat, and Mr. Crandall offered her a warmer one. "Your sable is probably still hanging in the closet at Quercorum. I can get it to you by Friday."

"Tell me," she said, pouring his tea, "are my delphinium still in the garden there? They were so lovely, remember?"

"I—well, I'll inquire. There's no gardener these days, I believe. Only a skeleton staff at any of the houses."

The sable coat arrived promptly. She drew its dark splendor from the pink-enameled box and saw that there was a note. "Delphinium all present and accounted for," wrote Mr. Crandall. "My office is looking around for some house help, including a gardener. I'm assuming that you plan to spend part of next summer at Quercorum? I always thought you liked it the best of your residences."

At night, her bedlights carefully extinguished, her ears alert for a possible intruder, she lay imagining the scene in the magazine—the great house, the tall blue flowers, the man with the sensitive mouth in the background—with a different woman standing where the embittered Mrs. Porter had stood, a woman who, smiling and serene, reached out a hand to her husband to draw him into the very center of the picture.

Just before Christmas, Robert came to see her. The preparations had been long-drawn-out and ticklish, so she was ready for him, from the tension in her stomach to the bowl of holly on her table to the sapphire earrings that gave her courage. From noon on the appointed day, she sat by her window, watching a snowy stretch of walk that he was almost sure to traverse; and so she saw him before he saw her—a tall, thin man, limping, leaning heavily on a cane, being careful of the slippery walk. The face was still handsome, but so drawn that she was moved nearly to tears.

Because she had found honesty to be the best policy whenever she could afford it, the first thing she said to him was, "I didn't know you limped. Nobody told me."

"It's from the accident. Other people are used to it by now, so they wouldn't think to mention it to you. For a while I was not sure I would walk again."

"Both of us have changed," she said. "Oh, Robert, it was good of you to come." She did not offer to shake hands. Something in his manner made her think it inadvisable.

That first visit was brief, awkward, and the subsequent ones were hardly better. He avoided her eyes, retreated from any proximity, spoke in a constrained way. Sometimes they drove down to the village for lunch— he had to sign out for her permission to go, which seemed to amuse him a little—but he never suggested that he sign her out for a weekend, which he had the legal right to do and which Dr. Lindsay might well have permitted.

None of her conversational gambits worked out well. "Are you staying at Quercorum?" she asked.

"No. I'm staying in a house I bought a few years ago, up near Concord. Have a young married couple to do the chores for me."

"But Quercorum is quite close. Don't you like it there?"

"Under the circumstances, no."

The forbidding tone in his voice always scared her off, and she could think of nothing safe to say, and their visits would end in painful silence.

"Mr. Crandall says the Gregory Porter thing is settled," she told him one afternoon.

"I know. Greg came to thank me, and I told him I had nothing whatever to do with it."

"You did, though. Indirectly."

"I'm glad it wasn't taken to court. We wouldn't have had a good press."

"If things work out as I hope, and if you take full charge of my affairs for me—"

"That would be quite impossible," he said, sharply. "Crandall said something about that, and I refused, unequivocally." The only hopeful sign was that he kept coming—once a week, twice, three times.

"I think you're getting a *little* used to me," she said. "Do I still seem like a stranger to you?"

"You're always charming these days. Which makes you quite a stranger indeed."

"I know I behaved unbearably to you but, thank God, I don't remember a lot of it. Since you haven't the advantage of a bad memory, I can only hope you'll forgive me, eventually."

"I didn't mean to be caustic. I was stating a fact."

"Then I'll state a fact, too. I regret most of the past. Except our marriage. I'll never regret that."

She expected that to please him, but he fell silent and left early again that day.

By the middle of February she was prickly with nerves and hard put to preserve the good-natured outgoing exterior the hospital seemed so fond of. Then, out of a magazine she picked up from her bedside table fluttered the second of the strange notes. The jagged black handwriting stared up at her from the floor until she bent, stiff with distaste, to pick it up.

Robert's no better than a murderer. It wasn't his fault he had no luck with it. Tell him so.
E.

Carefully she burnt the note in an ashtray. Then she walked out to ask the nurses on the floor whether they had seen anyone entering or leaving her room.

"No, Mrs. Porter. No one's gone by here, and they'd have to, to get to you."

"I think it would be a woman," she said, incautiously. "One of the other patients, maybe?"

"It certainly wouldn't be a patient. This isn't a free floor. Is something missing from your room?"

She saw that their eyes were intent, speculative. "Oh, no, no. Nothing like that. It's only—well, I found a magazine that I didn't recognize, and I thought someone might have left it for me—" She retreated in a flurry of excuses, but not soon enough. She had earned herself a black mark for the day, and Dr. Lindsay brought the matter up the next morning.

"Are you well enough acquainted with one of our women patients for her to *want* to visit you, Mrs. Porter?"

"Well, no. I speak to some of them in passing, but I don't know their names or anything. I just thought maybe—"

"What magazine was it?"

"Oh. Well, one of those picture magazines, I think."

"You seemed quite certain yesterday. Are you less certain now?"

She felt ill—dizzy, nauseated, a ringing in her ears. She had to summon her forces to be bold. "I am not paranoiac, Dr. Lindsay. I made an honest mistake, asked an idle question. To tell you the truth, I'm so upset over Robert's behavior that I don't know which way to turn. It makes me absent-minded and foolish, and I'm sorry."

That gave him something new to think about. "What about Robert? He seems quite devoted, to me. He'd come every single day, if we'd let him."

She clasped her hands. "Really? Is that really true?" The joy of it warmed her. The nausea receded. "Oh, Dr. Lindsay, you've made my day!"

"If he's being cautious, you can't blame him. It seems not to have worked out well, before."

"But it will this time," she said, confidently. "Because I know better now, don't you see?"

"*What* do you know? Let's talk about that."

But she could not talk about it satisfactorily without telling him that she was not really Ellen Porter, so she stumbled over his questions and was finally dismissed, feeling like a student who had abjectly flunked an important test.

She went straight to her telephone and asked Robert to come at once. "I'll meet you outside by the fountain near the parking lot," she said. "We can have some privacy there. I have some important questions I *must* ask you. Please prepare yourself to be honest, no matter what. Absolutely honest."

The air was lively with snowflakes, and the day was cold. She waited by the fountain, huddled in her sable, squinting against the wind. A bad setting for a very serious conversation, but it was one that simply must not be overheard—by the real Ellen Porter or anyone else. (For surely one of the things the mysterious notes revealed was that the writer had some method of surveillance.) Robert arrived on the dot, his eyes curious and worried, and she didn't bother to greet him.

"I've run out of time," she said, "so I must ask these things openly. First, do you think you could ever be—well—fond of me?"

He answered without hesitation. "I'm fond of you now, and I don't in the least want to be. At first I felt nothing because you seemed like a stranger to me, but then I saw that you were being the way you were when you were sixteen, before all the bad temper and money-grubbing set in. I wouldn't have thought you could ever be that way again, but you are."

"Good. Second question. If I had died in that accident, would you have been tried for my death?"

"Yes. I nearly was, anyway. The police tried hard to make a case—at least of manslaughter—but I was laid up for so long, and there were no immediate witnesses, and you *didn't* die—"

"Did you want me to?" she asked, gently. "Was it attempted murder?"

For the first time he looked directly at her, in a long silence. "Yes," he said, steadily. "I meant to kill us both. I hoped you wouldn't remember that, but I'm glad you have. I can't tell you how it's weighed on me all these years."

"I thought we should get that question out of the way. Does anyone else know?"

"I tried to tell Arthur Crandall, but he said he didn't want to listen to it. He said that when two people were angry and fighting each other for the steering wheel, there was no telling who was more at fault. But I know that I aimed us straight at that abutment, and that, if you hadn't managed to turn us the least bit—"

She put her hand over his lips. "Forget about it. It doesn't matter anymore."

"Now you can understand why I felt so guilty, especially when you were being friendly and dear—"

She kissed his stricken face. "We mustn't waste a minute on regret. That's one lesson I've been taught in this hospital. What we should be doing is making plans for the next twenty years or so. Shall we begin by going to Quercorum for Easter?"

He put an arm around her waist, fell into step beside her, his eyes alight. "Better yet, why don't we go down there this weekend? I could ask my young married couple to come along to do the cooking. Remember how beautiful those big oaks were in the winter? I suppose there are still seventy-nine of them. I counted them once, if you recall."

She blinked away tears of happiness. "I'd love to go there. I'd forgotten about the oak trees—"

"But that's where the place gets its name. 'Quercus' means 'oak,' in Latin. Maybe the horses are still there, too. Not that I'll ever be able to ride again—"

In their absorption, they nearly collided with Dr. Lindsay, on his way to the parking lot. "Well," said the doctor dryly. "It looks like an early spring." They both talked to him at once, about the necessary pass for the weekend at Quercorum, about how wonderful it was that Ellen was so well, about the miracle of being given a second chance at happiness. Dr. Lindsay agreed with them on everything. There was reluctance in his eyes, but he knew when he was outnumbered.

As she and Robert continued their stroll, she was careful, however, to keep a line of trees between the hospital windows and themselves. The real Ellen Porter, seeing her husband thus engrossed, might not be completely magnanimous.

* * * *

On the spring morning when Mrs. Porter left the hospital for good, holding her husband's arm, talking to the circle of doctors and nurses that attended her, Wally thought she looked great. Very happy. Animated. Beautiful, almost, though that was a funny word to use about a woman who was fiftyish. He traded smiles with her—he had said his own farewells the day before—and then stood back and just watched, out of the way of the fuss the hospital apparently felt it had to make over a member of the Founding Family.

Thus he saw a strange little occurrence that no one else appeared to see. He saw Mrs. Porter, still laughing and talking and without once lowering her eyes from the faces around her, reach into her purse, bring out a small notebook, write something on one of the pages, tear the page from the notebook, fold it carefully, and put pen and notebook away, retaining the folded note in her gloved hand. There was nothing odd about any of that, except her cleverness at writing without looking; but five minutes later, just before she entered her car, she looked down at the folded paper, recoiled as if she'd seen a tarantula, and threw the little piece of paper, still folded, into the gutter.

So I'm imaginative, he thought, I make things up, why would anybody be repelled by something he had just written? And when, after the car had driven off and the godspeed group dispersed, he picked up the folded paper and read it, he was still puzzled. In an angular, black handwriting, the note said:

> I am content to remain here, having set you free. You are rid of me for good. Be happy. I never was.
> E.

A strange little note, but not a repulsive one. And, of course, Mrs. Porter hadn't even read it—though, since she had written it, she must know what it said.

Wally, old boy, he told himself, pull yourself together. This note could not possibly have been written by Mrs. Porter, it's a crazy little note and must have been handed to her by another patient; the hand is quicker than the eye, there must have been *two* pieces of paper, and you're mistaken about the whole business.

For a moment he thought of showing the note to Dr. Lindsay, as a psychological curiosity, but it was getting near dinnertime and he was hungry. He pitched the paper into a trash can and walked down the hill toward home, whistling. The days when the sick recovered were the best of days.

✗

www.ingramcontent.com/pod-product-compliance
Lightning Source LLC
Chambersburg PA
CBHW050826180626
46814CB00004B/1478